There was a moment of tension in the room as Beverlee and Sonia examined the battle plans and then each other. Then Sonia cracked a smile at Bev and nodded her curly dark head at me. "Count me in, Kelsey. It's time we three did something to stop that little twerp, Taffy Foster."

"I'm in too," Beverlee added. There was a sparkle in her eyes.

Like I said, desperate women take desperate chances. Sick and tired of being the Ugly Ducklings at Balboa, powerless and overlooked, we decided to take some action to assert ourselves and make a point. Only we didn't bargain on danger until it was too late to back out.

ELLEN LEROE lives in San Francisco. She is the author of *Confessions of a Teenage TV Addict*, also available from Pacer Books.

The Plot Against the Pom-Pom Queen

ELLEN LEROE

Pacer BOOKS FOR YOUNG ADULTS

BERKLEY BOOKS, NEW YORK

for Beverly H. Day,
who taught me
the meaning of friendship

The Plot Against the Pom-Pom Queen

 **one**

The first time Taffy Foster called me Pig Woman in front of her friends, I vowed I'd get thinner.

The second time she did it, I vowed I'd get even.

She didn't really *call* me Pig Woman as much as grunt it in true swinelike fashion after I made my entrance center stage in the school auditorium and nervously walked down the runway. The other girls in Mannequin Club—fresh, dewy-eyed Cheryl Tiegs types and Diet Pepsi commercial beauties—had modeled their outfits and now waited on the side of the stage for my entrance. I was to be the last number in the show.

"And wrapping up our fashion presentation today is the crisp little nautical look we'll be seeing so much next spring," cooed our modeling club advisor, Mrs. Hammer. "And wearing the ensemble of smart white pants and adorable middy blouse is Kelsey Marshall."

All right. So maybe white isn't exactly the most flattering color for an ex-Ms. Chubbette, but it can't look too bad. Oh please, I prayed as I swayed down the little runway as gracefully as possible, don't let me trip or stumble. I'll just die from humiliation and public disgrace, I know I will. All parts of my body seemed to function correctly as I remembered to make my first turn midstage while smiling fashion-model style. Then, disaster struck. There was a slight rustling in the front rows, and I heard it distinctly—the unmistakable sounds of a huge pig grunting obscenely. In the shocked sea of silence that followed, the grunts got louder and I stopped, my mind not working for several seconds, the smile still fixed to my face. I peered blindly out into the mass of faces.

Is this how it feels to be hit by a bullet? Or to be Marie Antoinetted by the friendly French guillotine?

I located the culprit easily enough. Taffy Foster—golden-haired, cheerleader-prototype Taffy Foster—surrounded by her inevitable clique of Pretty People, stifling hysterical giggles and making those vicious but realistic piglike grunts. I wanted to scream. I wanted to wrench the heavy podium off the stage and hurl it into the audience right at her head in Incredible Hulk-like retaliation. But it was too late. Already, widening ripples of laughter had broken out here and there. Several kind teachers were trying resignedly to shush the offenders; it was no use. The damage had been done. The giggles blossomed into an epidemic of chuckles, chortles, and outright guffaws, swelled into a veritable tidal wave of side-splitting hoots of laughter at my expense. Kelsey Marshall: Middy Magnitude in White, Her Fashion Fatness.

Pig Woman. I could sense, if not actually hear, the words

2

being tossed lightly, like a beach ball, among Taffy Foster's friends. To make matters worse, I saw Cal Lindsey poke his head through the side door of the auditorium, a puzzled look on his face, as the laughter spilled into the hallway. Of all the cruel twists of fate! Of all the rotten pieces of timing, to have the love object of practically every girl in Balboa High witness my embarrassing scene. Cal Lindsey: my idol, my raison d'être, the male of my dreams in Technicolor and 3-D. Over six feet tall, a broad-shouldered, blond-haired Adonis, Cal Lindsey possessed a gunslinger squint along with a baby-sweet dimple that tore the heart right out of me. What a combination —that Clint Eastwood tough-guy brashness and macho softened by the vulnerable smile and warm laugh.

Cal Lindsey was so sexy that girls under seventeen would not be admitted to his classes without an accompanying parent. So attractive that, after seeing him, Robert Redford and Burt Reynolds would rush to make appointments with their therapists to bolster their sagging egos. So athletic and gifted that *Sports Illustrated* would want to put him on their cover— and then devote an entire issue to his prowess in a number of sports. Describe him any way you want to, physically and emotionally he was the image of perfection—the sex symbol of the senior class.

Because he was staring at me, I started moving again: the statue coming to life, Marie Antoinette's guillotined head being reintroduced to her body. I actually managed to laugh along with the audience and ended up standing by the other models. Mrs. Hammer threw me a quick grateful look and wrapped up the program.

I wanted to shrivel and die. I wanted to scrunch up like wrinkled aluminum foil and throw myself away in the school's litter basket. *Pig Woman.*

I scanned the audience before our principal let the masses out. My eyes lit on the golden-haired wonder. I stared at her with suspiciously tear-bright eyes and a dagger up my middy sleeve. I'll get you for this, Taffy Foster. Ah yes, you'll pay for this little deed today. You'll pay. But even as I was figuring out the size and shape of the voodoo doll I'd construct—with the prerequisite synthetic blonde hair and the pert, upturned nose and slanted, almond-shaped green eyes—I knew I had no real ammunition in my arsenal. At least, none that would wound, or even dent, the perfectly formed armor of Taffy Foster, or Cotton Candy as I called her. The problem was, she was too pretty. And prettiness, I was fast learning, spelled *power*. Prettiness got you all the little perks in life that most other girls couldn't command: like having school doors held open for you by several drooling guys; like never having to audition for Pom-Pom girls, the elite set of cheerleaders; like never having to go hungry for boys to take you to dances or mixers. Hungry? That was a laugh. For Taffy Foster and the Pretty People, there were usually too many admiring males floating around, if you could believe that.

I couldn't have, until I transferred here as a sophomore last year. About that first school year—the less said, the better. Certainly I made good grades and managed to find three good friends in the bargain (one of them actually a male!), but mainly, I was a nonentity: quietly slipping in and out of unfamiliar classrooms, keeping my voice down and my profile low. Unfortunately, not as low as I liked. My bathroom scale attested to that. Much as I yearned to be sylphlike, one-calorie-soft-drink-conscious, the oh-so-elegant thin machine displayed provocatively in leotards in dance class or in skimpy little sweaters and jeans, I was not the ballerina, but the tutu. Because I was slightly plump and far more curvaceous than

4

I wished, watching my diet should have been a full-time occupation for me. Of course, it didn't help to have a stylish stout for a mother—someone who equated maternal love with generous portions of pasta, potatoes, and pancakes—but more about her later. Right now I was too wounded to think of anyone, or anything, except Taffy Foster . . . and of course, Cal Lindsey.

The one followed the other, automatically and literally. They were both star-bright luminaries of Balboa High, the acknowledged leaders of the school. Taffy's dazzling Playmate of the Month attributes and cruel mannerisms only served to ensnare her men more totally. This was yet another fact I was learning: Men find nice girls boring, too predictable; while the irrational, selfish all-for-me beauties rev men's engines from first to fourth gear immediately. Consideration is out, heartlessness is in. No brain she, Taffy Foster had an IQ of 6. Perhaps I'm exaggerating. She might have had an IQ of 10. That was why she couldn't join the Mannequin Club, her grade point average was too low. Yet she managed to pass all her courses with a lot of help from her more intelligent friends. She prowled the halls, an untamed lioness, blonde mane full and blown dry, dipping seductively below an eye with *Cosmopolitan* magazine bewitchery, green eyes shaded expertly to look twice their size, full pink lips glossed and licked to look pouty and innocent and, at the same time, streetwise Lolita. Most males in her path were goners. One smile, one husky word from her lips picked up those helpless boys like lint in the path of a killer vacuum cleaner. And much too soon, they were chewed up and collected in her ever-growing dustbag. Very few escaped that fate. Very few wanted to.

Except for Cal Lindsey. (Cal Lindsey, beautiful three syllables, how I loved to say his name.) This is why I felt myself get all hot and flushed just thinking about His Studship. He was one of the few males I knew who seemed immune to the Blonde Bombshell. Correction: Blank Bombshell. Oh, he noticed her all right. What man wouldn't? She seemed to be prime filet cut surrounded by a mass of chain-store Quarter Pounders. But he never asked her out. He never waited for her, doglike, outside her classes like so many others did, never invited her to watch him play on his teams (football, track, lacrosse . . . you name it) He never sat across from her in the cafeteria or even walked down the hall with her. He acknowledged her, if at all, with a brief, impassive glance. Cal Lindsey was a sex symbol, all right, but of the Greta Garbo school. He wanted to be alone, and most of the time he was.

It was driving Taffy crazy. Here was the one guy at Balboa who was her peer, who was *entitled* to share her wealth, and he didn't want it. How could that be? It confused Taffy. The Brontosaurus Brain went into fits, but what could she do?

Early in my junior year, I made the fatal mistake of grinning knowingly at my friends when Taffy was once again ignored by Cal Lindsey. She caught the grin, and the all-too-obvious message, and fixed me with the most malevolent look ever to come down the pike since the Wicked Witch of the West. It was embarrassing to the reigning Duchess of Deliciousness to have a blob like Kelsey Marshall and her two equally nonexistent friends finding *her* an object of scorn. She stood barely ten feet away from me that rainy September morning, quivering with anger, curling and uncurling her perfectly manicured fingers. She looked me up and down and hissed, "Pig Woman." Her small circle of Pretty People smirked.

A hot flush immediately crept up my neck to my cheeks.

What if other people had heard her? What if—God forbid—Cal Lindsey had been here! Too upset to make a comeback, I just stood there, a speechless mass. Taffy Foster flicked back her Barbie-doll strands of hair and swept off down the hallway, accompanied by her giggling retinue, her good mood restored.

Now, nearly two months later, the same speechless mass stood shaking in the small backstage dressing room. The other girls in the Mannequin Club were quickly getting out of their outfits and into their school clothes. By their averted eyes and subdued manner, I could tell they were as embarrassed as I was and didn't know how to approach me. One or two smiled tentatively in my direction, then scurried out the door.

What do you say to a Pig Woman?

Say, who was that sailorwoman I saw you with last night?

That was no woman, that was a pig!

Mrs. Hammer, a faded Jane Russell look-alike, nervously adjusted her glasses and came over to hang up my outfit. My naughty nautical ensemble.

"Never mind, dear," she murmured, folding the white pants carefully on the hanger. "It was all just a—a joke. Just done in fun."

If that was a joke, then the sinking of the *Titanic* must have reduced Mrs. Hammer to happy tears. The woman meant well, however, so I nodded briefly and started brushing my hair. Anything to avoid walking out that door into the whirling vortex of Balboa High—with its laughter, its whispers, its stories of beached whales in white impersonating sailors.

I moved to the mirror and stared at myself. A somewhat short, plump, baby-faced girl with chin-length, straight black hair, wide-set, Bambi-like eyes, and a shattered expression peered back at me. Not an ugly girl, not an ugly body, just lackluster, blah. Granted, I had clear, creamy skin and expressive hazel eyes, but the features, rather regularly formed, almost delicate, seemed lost in the overripe contours of my chin and baby fat. My hands and feet were small-boned and graceful, but no one notices articulated fingers or a sexy instep when the main bulk of your body quivers to a dead stop in front of him, demanding attention. The wrong kind of attention.

I was a high school junior with a problem. Sweet Sixteen and never been kissed and all on account of my weight. Or so I believed. Oh, I hated looking like this, hearing the comment: "You'd be so pretty, if only you'd lose a few pounds." And boys? That was a laugh. Apart from my one friend at school, John Perry (J.P.) Curtin, I really didn't relate to boys in the male/female way. I didn't know how. And it was driving me crazy, because since September, I had developed this overwhelming *thing* for Cal Lindsey. Call it a passion, an obsession. I couldn't concentrate on my schoolwork, I couldn't even talk rationally to John Perry anymore. Instead, I loved to walk through the halls with my two friends, Sonia and Beverlee, the invisible student bodies, searching for Cal Lindsey, being struck dumb with joy when he appeared. An entire day was made on just such an appearance. But I could only do it with a low profile.

And now Taffy Foster was out gunning for me. And if she ever discovered how much I was in love with Cal Lindsey, I just knew she'd spoil everything for me, and make me as well as Cal the laughingstocks of the whole school. With that comforting thought tucked away in my brain, I finished making myself presentable, and then with my hand on the door, I paused. I took a deep breath and said a little prayer. Please don't let anyone laugh at me behind my back. A sudden strange feeling came over me. If I believed in ESP or premonitions, I would have said it felt like Taffy Foster walking over my grave, like something unthinkable and awful was about to happen to me—and I was helpless to stop it. Something to do with Cal Lindsey.

Then the little cold shiver left and I shook myself. This was not a horror movie location, but fairly suburban Crestwood Heights, a sunny California community approximately twenty miles south of San Francisco. I was even grinning slightly as I pushed open the door and took a step into the busy corridor . . . to come face to face with the bane of my existence—Taffy Foster! She was gliding by, head held high, a vixen in pinks and plums, the tantalizing strawberry ice-cream sundae all boys would pay 9,000 calories for. From the corner of my eye, I could see my friends Sonia and Beverlee rushing up behind me, young mother lionesses ready to defend their cub. But Taffy didn't speak to me or look at me. She merely strode by, her coterie in tow, with just the tiniest of smirks on her face. But as she turned the corner, the fragment of a grunt came wafting back and then, roars of laughter.

Pig Woman.

And I burst out crying as Sonia put her arm around me, and she and Beverlee led me down the hall to a more secluded spot.

"I hate her," I sobbed, blowing my nose in Beverlee's proffered handkerchief. "I really loathe her! Just because she's the Pom-Pom Prima Donna doesn't mean she can humiliate me in public and get away with it."

Sonia looked glumly at me.

"Forget about it, Kelsey. Just try to ignore her. You'll see, within a short time, she'll stop picking on you."

"When—in two weeks? Two months? No, Sonia. I've had

it. This time Taffy Foster's gone too far. I don't know how or when, but I vow I'm going to do something."

I stood up straighter, my shoulders rigid with determination. Unfortunately, the rest of my body was quivering. But the eyes of my friends were round and scared.

"I vow on—on Cal Lindsey's sex appeal—that I will get even with that girl if it takes all year. But when I do, watch out!"

✴ two

I called an emergency meeting of UDA the very next afternoon. UDA stood for Ugly Ducklings Anonymous, an elite and highly exclusive membership among Balboa's finest. No one dated in UDA. No one had a boyfriend. Those were the requirements. Actually, there were only three of us, and although we laughed at the title and at our endless talks and fantasies about Cal Lindsey and the other males at school, our motto should have read Misery Loves Company.

Now Sonia and Beverlee gathered at my house after school that November afternoon and talked about one thing: revenge.

"Drop it," Sonia warned me, sitting on the floor, propped against the living-room sofa. From that angle, she resembled a gangly rag doll. "If you value your life at all, you'll forget you ever made that ridiculous vow yesterday. It's not going to get you anywhere, except in more trouble."

"Sonia's right, Kel," chimed in Beverlee from the sofa. "There's no way you can fight Taffy Foster and win."

I stood up in one miserable motion. "Why? Because she's some sort of protected princess? Because she's so pretty? You think being pretty makes her invulnerable to the things in life that hurt you or me?"

No one spoke for a minute or two, but they answered me by their silence. Y-E-S. Beverlee caught Sonia's eye and shook her reddish blonde head. Giving up already. There was no fight in either of them. For some reason, that infuriated me more.

"Well, I don't believe that," I said sharply. A little too sharply? Methinks the piglet doth protest too much. "Taffy Foster is a real person—"

"I think you mean real plastic," interrupted Sonia.

"—and not some kind of god. I mean, she does think and feel—to a limited degree, I'll admit. And we have seen her actually duck into the bathroom, so she must have natural functions and outlets."

Beverlee gave a short, humorless laugh. "Maybe she goes in there to recharge her robot batteries."

"All right. All right. We all know Cotton Candy is fluffery personified. But we also know that beneath the pretty plastic is an ugly, scared person."

"If that's ugly, I'll take grotesque any day," Sonia snorted.

"And scared? C'mon, Kelsey!" Beverlee arched a disbelieving eyebrow.

"You bet. Why else would she go gunning for me? Think

12

about it. I'm not just an irritant to her. Oh no. I get under her skin. I point out the distressing fact that she ain't perfect—she can't get Cal Lindsey. She's like the emperor in that Hans Christian Andersen story, "The Emperor's New Clothes," and I'm the little honest boy. She's deathly afraid that any minute I might scream, 'Hey, the Pom-Pom Queen isn't as great as she lets on she is. She may be a loser like the rest of us.' She's scared, believe me."

"The scared part we can believe, but with hesitation. But being a loser? No way. Taffy Foster has nothing to lose."

I paced up and down on our plush Antron nylon carpet, stepping over Sonia's sprawled, thin legs. An exciting thought was pushing into my mind, and for once it didn't have anything to do with food. Now if I could only make my two friends see, well, it might change our whole junior year.

I whirled to face them. "Look, if Taffy Foster has nothing to lose, then neither do I. Right? I mean, what's worse than being called Pig Woman in public in front of several hundred laughing kids? How much lower could I sink? At least I kept my dignity yesterday. At least I didn't *hog* center stage."

"Oh, please," Beverlee groaned, hurling a pillow at me. "Not your weird sense of humor now. This is too serious."

"Why is it?" I demanded. "That's just what our sexy little friend wants us to believe. She *wants* me to get all hot and bothered about her latest dumb smear campaign. You know, she's just lucky I didn't *squeal* on her."

Muffled giggles from Sonia and head shaking from Beverlee. At this point, my mom, Mrs. Margaret Marshall, poked her coiffured head into the living room.

"Hi, girls. I have some goodies for you. Shall I bring them in now or are you at a secret part of your meeting?"

13

My mother would have to interrupt at the crucial stage of our discussion. But then, she had this divining-rod aptitude for sniffing out gossip and pouncing on it. The woman was a walking *National Enquirer.* She was an irritant, a gusher, an emotionally smothering mom at times, but she was also my strongest fan and most loyal subject. No other parent I knew in Crestwood Heights could watch the Miss America pageant every year and turn to guests and say, "Yes, that Miss Ohio sure is pretty, but our Kelsey is much prettier!" No other parent in this community had a studio-size portrait of her offspring religiously positioned on the color TV set with a small votive candle beside it. And a number of Polaroid snapshots of baby-fatted Kelsey in all stages of growth propped up on coffee tables, mantels, and the smooth top of the refrigerator.

"OK, Mags." I sighed, pointing to the coffee table. "Bring the munchies in. I think we could use a break."

While everyone bustled around, spreading napkins and loading their plates, I took a moment to look at my two closest friends objectively. What I saw disturbed me. Although both girls were not unattractive, they bore the stigmas of being so. Their personalities did not say "Pretty."

Sonia was tall, and while structurally arresting, she didn't resemble Audrey Hepburn as much as the Eiffel Tower. Make that the Leaning Tower of Pisa. She slumped to one side all the time, trying to disguise her five-foot–ten-inch height. Instead, she called attention to it. She had short brown hair, quite pretty, that framed an expressive face. She had fabulous Sophia Loren eyes, but you'd never know it. Huge tortoise-shell-rimmed eyeglasses hid her best feature. She was all legs and arms—an awkward filly. But her personality and compassion for other people made her a winner.

Beverlee, on the other hand, already sipping a Coke, sat curled up like a frightened kitten. Tiny, soft-looking, and vulnerable, she viewed the world with an air of apology. "Oh, I'm sorry," she'd breathe fifty times a day to fifty different people for fifty different reasons. None of which, I may add, merited an excuse or an apology. Beneath the shy facade, Beverlee was really a dynamite actress. One day in English she astounded us all by breathing life into a Shakespearean monologue. Naturally, she apologized afterward for giving such a poor reading. I could have wrung her self-effacing kitten's neck.

So here they both sat, two talented people, making excuses for themselves and slumping through life afraid to reach out and take a risk. Join Drama Club, in Beverlee's case. Or lend organizational and people-oriented skills to School Community Service, in Sonia's. School Community Service was a select group of students who were chosen on the merit of their grades and behavior to aid the teachers and administrative staff with office work and confidential teaching material. The second week of September, the school's assistant principal, Mr. Del Maio, had asked Sonia if she wanted to join, but his offer was promptly rejected. The reason?

"Kelsey, think about it! I stand out like a sore thumb wherever I go, and well, working in the Administrative Office, I'd stick out even more. Towering over the teachers, messing up all their assignments. It's a big responsibility, and I just *know* I couldn't handle it."

She could handle it. And she'd be great at it. Just like Beverlee would be a smash in Drama. Or even reading the morning announcements over the Balboa PA system. With her voice and theatrical flair, she'd grab the attention of the whole school in record time. The whole school . . . My God.

15

Think of the fun you could have with a job like that. Or even working on School Community Service. Mimeographing teachers' confidential papers— Who knows what you might be asked to copy some day? Study outlines, homework assignments, or even tests! And helping Bat Lady DeCarlo with attendance records and grade scores. A smart person could wield a lot of power in the right position. And being a Pom-Pom girl wouldn't even come close to the knowledge and power you could have.

Slowly, oh-so-carefully, my mind started clicking. Vague possibilities began sliding into place. Maybe there was a way to beat Cotton Candy at her own game. But it would take diabolical cunning and a criminal mind to figure out a plan, plus the self-confidence to carry it through. Not to mention involved, loyal henchmen. Squinting at Bev and Sonia in my living room, I suddenly saw them as two-thirds of The Three Musketeers. Courageous, intelligent, and able to leap tall buildings in a single bound. The Clark Kent, Lois Lane, and Jimmy Olsen of downtown Metropolis. Self-assurance personified.

Then Beverlee lifted her pale blue eyes to mine and smiled nervously. "Why are you staring at me like that, Kelsey? Did I spill Coke on the sofa? Oh, dear, I'm sorry. I can't think why I'm so uncoordinated or why I don't take better care, now where . . . ?"

Down went the great self-assurance plane in a blaze of fire and smoke. So much for the confidence part of the scheme. I shook my head sadly at my friend who was frantically searching her clothes and the sofa for telltale soda stains. This was going to be harder than I imagined. But for the sake of Ugly Ducklings Anonymous I wanted to try. Before Margaret got too comfortable with my friends, I shooed her away as gently as possible. It had to be done with as much tact as I could muster. If you hurt my mother's feelings and made her feel left out, she'd pout and bat her baby browns at you mistily for hours.

"OK. What's up?" Sonia put down her half-eaten Ding Dong and eyed me suspiciously. "I can almost see the wheels turning in your twisted brain. But if this is about Taffy Foster, I don't want to hear it!"

"Well, I do," Beverlee said, surprising us both. "Maybe Kelsey's thought up a safe way to bump her off. Y'know, like a perfect murder? Putting Vanish in her thermos or Drano in Taffy's cheerleading tights. Something quick and painless."

"Drano is painless?" Sonia sat up, her analytical mind already beginning to function over this hypothetical problem. "No, you'd need another chemical or drug to make someone die painlessly. Besides, Drano needs liquid to do its stuff. Just sticking her leg in it isn't going to do anything except give her a rash or burn."

"The label doesn't say so," Beverlee said, pinching her kitten's face in concentration. "At least, I don't think it does. I'm sorry, Sonia, but I think the skull and crossbones on the back mean—"

"Hold it!" I shouted, interrupting this futile dialogue. "If we're going to talk about the problem, let's talk about it seriously. I think I have the beginning of an idea, but I need your input. Are you at least willing to listen?"

At the sight of my somber expression, they both quieted down, although I thought I heard Sonia mutter, "I still think this whole revenge bit is crazy!"

"I don't like it any more than you do, but then you're not

17

being crucified in public as a Pig Woman," I reminded her. "Although as my friends, you're guilty by association, so maybe you can qualify as piglets. Or part of the litter. Now here's what I'm thinking."

I outlined as briefly as possible my thoughts about the hidden potential in working on the PA system or in the Administrative Office at school. About how there seemed to be a hidden, untapped source of power that someone could use if he or she wanted to get even with someone. At the end of my rather vague recital, Sonia and Beverlee exchanged puzzled looks. They turned blank faces to me.

"So what does all this cloak-and-dagger stuff have to do with Taffy Foster?" ever-practical Sonia asked. "It seems to me Beverlee's Vanish or Drano plot's the more logical way to go if you're taking direct action."

"Yeah, I don't get it, Kel," Beverlee agreed. "I mean, what does the Balboa PA crew or the School Community Service have to do with you?"

"Not me," I smiled sweetly. "With you two."

"Us!"

"That's right. Just listen for a second. Beverlee, if you got into the PA crew, you could have access to all the important messages and information and scheduling of events going on in the school. You'll know when the Pom-Pom girls meet and where. You'll know about some of the cheerleading competitions and games before Taffy does."

"So?"

"So," I said slowly, feeling my way in the revengeful dark, "so maybe if you're writing the announcement for somebody else to read, you can, oh, translate it a little differently. So that it would throw somebody off. Or you can read a message correctly, and if I know the day and morning you'll be reading it, I can keep Cotton Candy from hearing it."

Sonia looked up. "What good does that do?"

"None if it's a general announcement. But if it has to do with an all-important competition, and Taffy misses it, the whole cheerleading squad will be furious. Especially if her excuse is a weak one. And with her dear little friends against her, we begin to crack her defenses, chip away her armor. We start small, then go on to bigger things."

Now I had their rapt attention. The very air sizzled with excitement like fried chicken in the pan. I thrust the tantalizing image of food from my mind and concentrated on putting across my case. It wasn't too difficult now that the concept of power had been introduced. Power in the hands of the Ugly Ducklings—an unheard-of thought.

"And what about me, Kel? What can I do?" Sonia asked. She tucked her long legs in and unconsciously thrust her shoulders back. My God, if this plot worked, I might transform three girls, not just one. It was a weird, almost frightening idea.

"Sonia, remember when Mr. Del Maio asked you to join School Community Service? Do you think you could reapply at this late date?"

"I don't know. I guess so. They're always looking for helpers in Administration. But why the office? Isn't that too far in the back lines for any action?" There was a distinct droop to her lips, but I had never seen Sonia's face so animated. For that matter, I had never seen Beverlee look so impenitent and cocky, the very opposite of her usual apologetic self.

"School Community Service is a perfect place to start our subversion," I told Sonia. "Calls come in to students all the time, and Mrs. Malachi trots all over delivering messages. Don't you think she'd enjoy a helper so she won't wear out those lace-up tennis numbers she wears? And what if the message was for T. Foster—maybe something romantic from C. Lindsey to meet him somewhere, somewhere nice and public where as many kids as possible can see the show. Maybe the message could lead her to believe that he wants to ask her to something, so that when she approaches him, all dewy-eyed and excited, his unexpected rebuff will throw her into a tailspin. And then she's made an absolute ass of herself in front of her friends and best of all, in front of Cal Lindsey."

"You're a genius!" Sonia breathed, then snapped her fingers. "Wait a minute! Let's not forget that I'll be helping teachers with their work plans and teaching assignments. And I'll be so good and trustworthy that maybe, just maybe, I'll get myself assigned to some of Taffy's instructors. Think of what I could do with her test papers! Or her homework! And you, Bev, on the PA system going out loud and clear to the whole school. 'This special request goes out to the only boy I really love. To you, Cal, from your ever adoring and always empty-headed Taffykins.' Oh God, what a scream! What an absolute scream!"

She dissolved in helpless giggles, and Beverlee joined in the happy hysterics moments later, rolling off the sofa while mimicking Taffy Foster's whiney, high-pitched voice. I smiled, but couldn't get into the mood. My mind was jumping like overheated popcorn. And all these disturbing thought kernels kept coming to the surface. Danger! they exploded in my brain. Look out. You're playing with Taffy Foster. This isn't just a game. More than anything I wanted to talk with my friend John Perry, who seemed to understand me so well and who would tell me what to do. Tomorrow over lunch he'd sit down with me and reassure me that my little plan would work. That the Pig Woman could actually get the better of the Pom-Pom Queen.

✳ three

"I know you're not brilliant, Kelsey, but I really didn't think
you had a birdbath for a brain," said my oh-so-reassuring
friend John Perry at lunchtime the next day. "I mean, you just
don't have it in you to be a game player, unless revenge has
suddenly become your major talent. And I don't see you like
that. I don't see you that way at all."

"Just how do you see me then, J.P.?" I asked coldly. "And
it'd better be good."

We were sitting outside on the stone ledge that rims the
school's quadrangle. I shifted angrily on the ledge and fanned
out my gauze peasant overblouse. That way, no one could
place bets on where my waistline was, and I wouldn't have to
walk around the school sucking in my stomach all day. My

mother had bought me the top as a surprise present. I had felt
pretty when I put it on this morning, like a Spanish señorita.
But now, checking out all the clingy tube tops and tight-fitting
T-shirts on the other girls, I just felt overblown and ridiculous.
I tried to shrink inside myself, but there was no room there,
either.

J.P. bit into his sandwich and surveyed my squirmings with
a clinical look in his eye. As much as I hated that look and the
words that would usually follow, I could always trust him to
tell the truth. The sunlight glinted off his soft brown hair and
his wire rims, and I could see my reflection in the lenses. It
was like putting your nose up to a Christmas tree ornament,
the big shiny ball kind, and seeing your features go all Silly
Putty.

J.P. crumpled his paper bag and banked the shot at a nearby
trash basket. It sailed neatly through the air and went in.
Bingo. That's typical, I sighed inwardly. Whatever J.P. set out
to do—methodically, carefully, scientifically—he usually suc-
ceeded in doing. That's why he made such a superb yearbook
editor, as well as a winning varsity swimmer. Once J.P. got
going, he didn't quit. Now he grinned at his basket and turned
back to me.

"I've got to be careful about what I say, don't I? I can tell
already by that wounded-deer look in your eyes."

I snorted. "More like wary deer. I'm not as bad as Margaret
in the sensitivity department." My mother was notorious, and
all my friends knew it.

"Not as sensitive, but close. Like mother, like daughter. But
listen, Kelsey . . ." He was all serious in a second, and my
stomach responded by tightening up. "I think you're a dy-
namic, sharp, funny girl who's ten times better than Taffy

23

Foster will ever be. Kinder, more caring about her friends, supportive, unselfish—"

"I'm still waiting to hear pretty," I interrupted with a kidding wink, but the humor was on the surface. "How about cute? I'll settle, at this point, for pert. But I forgot, pert usually takes a dainty, petite body, and that ain't me. So, okay, I'm not Miss Crestwood Heights, but God, J.P.! You make me sound like a dog. You know the spiel. You've heard it before. 'Oh, Kelsey? Hey, she's great. Really great. What a personality. What a smile! What—is she foxy? Hey, take my word for it, looks aren't everything. This girl is something else.' Well, thanks for all the nice adjectives, but no thanks. The only adjective I really want to hear just isn't on the menu. And I've had it up to here with the jovial fat person patter."

"Who said anything about jovial?" he said calmly, fixing me with those level brown eyes. "Who said anything about fat? You're the only person going around making a big deal out of something that shouldn't be a problem."

"Oh, really? Try telling that to beetle-brain T. Foster. She's the one who started this stupid vendetta in the first place!"

"Why don't *you* try telling her, Kel?"

"Me?" Shock jammed my mental airwaves and I could only stare open-mouthed at J.P., chocolate cupcake crumbs on my mouth.

He grinned and handed me a napkin. "That's right. Have you ever thought that you could probably get this all worked out if you confronted Taffy, alone? And then just talked to her honestly about your feelings and the current situation?"

"You're asking me, the person she regards as poison ivy, to go right up to her and ask her to open up, bosom buddy to bosom buddy and all that?"

He nodded his head.

I shook my head vigorously. "That's like asking the chicken to go up and introduce itself to the fox. Like having an old lady with a Social Security check in her frail, little hand strike up a conversation with a mugger. Talk about a stupid suggestion!"

"Is it any more stupid than spinning your wheels on a re-venge plot so complicated that the Count of Monte Cristo would be confused? At least it's dealing with the problem openly. Not this sneaky kid's game of getting even."

"So what you're telling me now is that you aren't going to help." I stared at my friend defiantly, but it was all an act. Inside I felt confused. I relied on J.P. to act as my moral compass, pointing me in the right direction and getting me out of dark, scary places. The kind of place I was in now. I think, looking back at the whole crazy mess, that if I had listened to J.P. at that moment, I might have saved myself from the cata-strophic chain of events that followed. If I had steeled myself to talk to Taffy, if I had apologized for smirking at her in front of Cal Lindsey in the first place, and if I had suggested we go our separate ways, everything might have ended on a soap-opera high. Cut and print! Two wary girls smile tentatively at each other and walk off arm in arm to discuss boys, biology, and bubble gum at the local malt shop.

But, as my heart weakened in secret relief and I resolved to ferret out Cotton Candy for the summit talk, there strode Cal Lindsey upon the scene: the sunshine of my life, the eggs Benedict of my existence! And events took a completely dan-gerous turn. It was downhill on Dead Woman's Curve from that point on, although he appeared at the moment to be heaven-sent. For this radiant angel in a royal blue Adidas jacket and faded cords actually veered in our direction. "Mercy," I breathed to myself in tremulous joy. The blond-headed god was moving right toward us.

I must have paled considerably because J.P. snapped under his breath, "Jesus, don't go fainting on me or anything! He's only coming over here to ask me about pictures for the yearbook. Now stop drooling and straighten up!"

I managed to slide my gauze peasant blouse off one dimpled shoulder and sit forward in what I considered a seductive pose. But the ruffled fabric on the front of the blouse was quivering because my heart was loudly, ferociously pounding in my chest. Cal Lindsey, Cal Lindsey, it boomed in racy rhythm. I stared at his Paul Newman-blue eyes that looked deliciously evil and experienced, and the blood in my virginal veins suddenly surged around my body at 180 miles per hour.

But Cal didn't notice me. I was safe to devour his face and body with uninhibited passion. He moved up to John Perry and then stopped, and propped one long, lean leg up on the ledge. His shoe was resting so close to my twitching fingers that I considered scraping a little dirt off to preserve in a special bottle.

"J.P., how goes it? Have you set a time and place for the photographer to take the pictures of the Fall Student Council officers?"

J.P. frowned a second and shook his head. "Bad news. Ted Keelias quit as chief photographer for the yearbook, and all my other guys aren't as qualified to take those pictures. I'm scouting around though. It shouldn't be more than another week or so before I get someone."

"Look, as soon as you do, let me know. I'll try to get all the officers assembled on a day's notice, but I'd like to have more time if possible." He turned to go, then swung his head around. "Hey, I meant to tell you. I caught your action at the meet against Bristol. Some really fine swimming, Curtin. I was impressed. I'd like to take you on sometime in a friendly competition. I could use a good workout in the water myself."

Instead of falling to his knees and slobbering his thanks, J.P. merely grinned and said he'd consider it. How could he be so cool and collected before this living representation of the spirit of Balboa High? It looked like my idol was all set to go this time; all my sharp digs into J.P.'s side were not giving him the message. But before I did anything more drastic, Fate with a capital *F* intervened. I believe that is the correct word to use, as *fatal* sounds so much like it, and what happened soon after took on the characteristics of that word. As Cal Lindsey turned to go, his leg knocked the pile of my books and the remains of my lunch off the ledge and onto the ground. In the ensuing flurry of activity, I furiously tried to hide my empty ice-cream carton, the two packs of Ding Dongs, the empty Good and Plenty box and the bag of corn chips for my midday snack while Cal gathered my books. He was flipping the last one over to hand to me when he stopped, as if jolted by something he'd seen. Puzzled, I reached out my hand to take the book, and then almost shrieked in outrage.

On the back of my trigonometry book was a huge Miss Piggy decal in fluorescent pinks and greens! It covered the entire back cover and depicted the vain little porcine sex symbol lifting her superb nostrils and batting her heavily made up eyes at Kermit in the background. The worst part was the words someone had scrawled beneath the picture: *Kelsey loves Kermit. Or is it Cal?*

"Wh-a-a-t?" Cal Lindsey stood there blankly, looking from my beet-red face to J.P.'s tight-lipped one. "Is this some kind of a joke?"

J.P. snatched the book away from my trembling hands and turned it over to hide the offensive cartoon. "The Cal's short for—for, uh, Calston Deprese, Balboa's illustrious social studies head. Right, Kel?"

I thought quickly. Calston Deprese was one of the least attractive teachers in the entire school and to admit to being turned on by this specimen would set me back eons in Cal Lindsey's eyes, but what else could I do? Better to have him think that I craved Deprese than that I harbored an undying love for *him*. So I mutely nodded and prayed that he'd accept this little white lie.

"Deprese, hmm?" he grinned. The dimple in his cheek appeared. For once I was too nervous to be mesmerized by it. "Ole Calston Deprese. I never thought I'd see the day when a student would actually fall for an old geezer like that. Lucky guy, though, to have you for his fan club. What's your name anyway, Kelsey what?"

The sun was in his eyes and he was squinting at me and he looked so handsome that I forgot what he had asked me until J.P. pinched my arm (a trifle viciously, I thought).

"Oh, uh, Marshall," I stammered. "Kelsey Marshall."

"Kelsey Marshall," he repeated thoughtfully, staring at me with an intense gaze. "Now why does that name sound so familiar to me? Funny how seeing that Miss Piggy sticker jogged my memory. Hmmmm. Oh well, can't think of it now. J.P., let me know about the photographer as soon as possible. And Kelsey, see ya later. Give my best to Deprese!"

He winked, gave a nonchalant wave, and quickly strode off into the sun. Immediately, two or three guys lounging by the fountain called out to him and collected around him, like iron attracted to a magnetic field. I sat down weakly and watched the ever-growing throng surge toward the building. This was all too much for me. My heart couldn't stand any more shocks. First having my dream man come within touching vicinity and then spotting that cruel decal on the back of my book. It was all Taffy's doing, I just knew it. Somehow she had maneuvered one of her little spies into decorating my book this morning while I was away from my desk or at the library. And since I didn't have trigonometry until last period, it was a cinch I probably wouldn't look at the book until then, and by that time, the decal would be in front of the whole class.

With increasing fury, I relived the embarrassment of seeing Cal Lindsey stare at the sickening words underneath Kermit the Frog. Oh God, what if J.P. hadn't been so quick in turning a potential disaster into nothing more than an awkward moment? I lifted grateful eyes to my friend, but he abruptly cut me off.

"Save it," he said coldly. "Just save it for now, OK?"

"Well, what's wrong with you!" I couldn't believe John Perry's abrupt mood change. We had been talking so easily before, and now he was the original Pac-Man: cold and robot-like. "J.P. What is your *problem*! I'm sorry you had to lie for me—is that it?—but I didn't think you'd get all uptight about such a minor thing."

He swung his compact swimmer's body off the seat and glared down at me. The twinkle that was usually in his clear brown eyes was gone, and even his boyish, good-natured features looked tight and hard.

"Listen to me, Marshall. You've got a problem all right— this stupid, petty, Miss Piggy vendetta between you and Taffy Foster. Yeah, she's a jerk and she shouldn't get away with embarrassing you by sticking decals on your books or grunting like a pig every time you're in public. But can't you do anything better about this so-called problem than think up a kid's revenge? And why make such a big deal over her feelings for Cal Lindsey? My God. That's the whole problem right there."

I jumped up, ready to take up the lance and the spear as soon as the magic name had been uttered.

"What problem?" I snapped. "I didn't realize Cal Lindsey had anything to do with my problem."

"Cal *is* your problem. Or one of them, my blind friend. You're just too dense to see it. You should see yourself around him. It's sickening. You behave like he's some god or something, and you're not worthy to carry his gym bag. Come off it. You just put yourself down and don't even know it."

"I know I do!" I cried, anger making my voice tremble. "You think I don't know what I look like—big, fat, bloated Kelsey? Every time I see Cal Lindsey or Taffy Foster, I want to die inside. They're so good-looking, so confident, so *thin*, that I feel like the Pig Woman Taffy keeps talking about."

John Perry shook his head quickly.

"You're not listening, Marshall—"

"Stop calling me Marshall!"

"You hear only what you want to hear. It's easy thinking of yourself as the Pig Woman. It's easy envying Taffy and drooling over Cal Lindsey like an eleven-year-old with a crush on Michael Jackson. But the hard part's not believing all this junk. Do you honestly see yourself as a blimp? Because if you do, you're crazy."

"You're the one who's crazy if you think I'm not fat, J.P.!"

"You're *not* fat, Kelsey. My God, you talk like you weigh two-hundred pounds instead of what? One-thirty or so? If you dressed differently, wore a different style, you'd look fine. Or better, if you got more involved at school, joined a club or something, you wouldn't have all the time to sit home with Momma and munch together. How about doing something

30

for a change and stop brooding about Taffy Foster? How about acting as my temporary photographer until I find someone permanent? I know you're good, your brother, Mike, taught you how to handle a camera, and he was top man on the staff just last year. Now there's something you've definitely got a flair for, so why not go for it? It'd be fun, and you'd be helping out a friend."

"What friend?"

I picked up my books slowly and stared at J.P. He looked different somehow, deflated and vulnerable. Our argument had left a strangeness between us that had never been there before, and I felt awkward. When he spoke again, his next question threw me and only pointed up how little I knew this boy.

"The Sadie Hawkins Dance is on Thanksgiving night—are you planning to go, Kelsey?"

"What do you mean, who would *I* ask? Who would want to go with me?" The school put on a dance after the Thanksgiving game every year, and the girls turned the tables and got to invite the boy of their choice. It was supposed to be a blast, from reports I had heard. I didn't go last year, and I certainly didn't intend to go this year. Me, ask someone as a date? Ridiculous.

"How about Cal Lindsey? Wouldn't you want to take him as your date?"

Now he must be joking! Yet his tone, his eyes, were dead serious, almost probing. There was something in his glance that I couldn't quite fathom, but I had never seen it before in John Perry.

"You know I couldn't ask Cal Lindsey. Why, that's crazy! He'd only laugh at me."

J.P. ran a hand through his light brown hair and shrugged.

31

"I know other guys who wouldn't. But you don't want to know that, do you? It scares you too much, doesn't it, Kelsey?"

"No, it doesn't scare me, J.P., because there are no boys out there waiting for me."

"And if there were . . . ?" J.P. searched my eyes, and I looked away, anxious to terminate this conversation.

"And if there were," I replied sarcastically before I could stop myself, "they'd have to be losers of the first order with huge eye cataracts. Now I've got to run. I've got English with Merrill, and she has a fit if you're a minute late." I shifted the books in my arms and turned.

J.P. said behind me, "You never answered me about the photography job for the yearbook."

"No," I said quickly. And started to walk away.

But his words caught up to me all too clearly. "Think about it, Kelsey. Take the weekend and think about the offer. I'll be anxious to hear what you decide."

But I had already decided what I was going to do. My fingers found the Miss Piggy decal and while I tried to rip it off the book, I knew that I was going to pay somebody back for this incident today. And I knew just who it was—and exactly how I'd do it.

✳ four

Without realizing it, John Perry had handed me the weapon for attack when he brought up the Sadie Hawkins Dance. This would be the perfect opportunity to crush the Pom-Pom Queen and stop her from tormenting me. But I had to act fast. That message beneath the **Miss Piggy** decal spelled *trouble*. Taffy sensed my fatal obsession for Cal and wanted to exploit it. And I couldn't allow that. For my sake, as well as my Star Prince's, nothing hurtful or malicious must touch him. Ever. And now that I had met him, actually spoken to His Radiance and got swept into the enticing whirlpool of those **devil eyes**, I was more hooked than ever.

I spent the next two days devising my little trap. Since it was a weekend, I had all the time in the world to sit at my desk and consider torment after torment. Mags grew slightly worried about me. When I didn't come down to the kitchen for our usual Friday night "party," she came up.

I usually anticipated these sessions (food orgies might be a more apt description), but this particular Friday night I was too busy contemplating my little plan to let junk food interrupt me. Naturally, Margaret was worried. She asked me how I was feeling; she produced a thermometer and tried to take my temperature. I pushed it and her away gently. I weakened gradually. Hot chocolate smells wafted upstairs to my room. She persuaded me to come downstairs for a little "snack."

I let Margaret fuss over me and make me a banana split in honor of regaining my appetite. As I started spooning the butterscotch sauce over the great gobs of ice cream, my dad blew in the house. When I say blew in, I mean that almost literally. The man resembled the energetic wolf in the old Disney cartoon that huffed and puffed until he blew the Three Little Pigs' houses down. In this case, it was two little pigs, but we were equally nervous.

Short, dark, and angular, with thinning gunmetal gray hair clipped military-close, a bristling black mustache and fierce blue eyes, he made an unusual partner for my rounded, soft, Pekinese-fluffy mother. Although my nervousness with my father stemmed from the fact that I wasn't a superstar daughter, I sensed that he truly loved me. He just couldn't articulate it. I was his only daughter, and while he was fiercely proud of my older brother, Michael, he was slightly in awe of me, his little girl. Whenever he came back from a sales trip, he would hold monosyllabic conversations with me, touching upon topics like school, my friends, my activities, like little pebbles thrown into a lake. *Ping! Ping! Ping!* Each topic lasted seconds and was soon lost in the deep water. Then he'd exhaust his stock of subjects and would grunt approvingly (all bases covered), and go back to either his unpacking or to his sales reports in the den. He was a sales manager for an important automotive accessories firm and traveled extensively throughout the western states.

Margaret must not have expected him back from his trip at that hour because she guiltily stopped eating and tried to hide the sumptuous junk-food spread behind the large centerpiece of dried flowers. But he didn't boom out as he usually did, "Caught you eating again, eh?" Instead, he threw his raincoat over a chair, put his small suitcase down by the dining-room table and absentmindedly kissed Margaret. Then he turned to me with a decided twinkle in those refrigerator-blue eyes and said, "What's this I hear about you and young Curtin? About time is all I can say!"

I made a gasping noise like I swallowed a goldfish. My father laughed.

"Cat got your tongue, eh? Only natural to be shy. Only natural. Right, dear?" He turned and smiled at Mags, who blinked nervously. "Of course, a shame I had to hear it secondhand from the father of John Perry, but well, kids get embarrassed. Afraid to tell the old man, eh?"

"Daddy," I said weakly, pushing away my sundae, "I don't know what you're talking about. What was I too embarrassed to tell you?"

"Why, that you and John Perry are going to this dance at school—y'know, the Sadie Hoskins—er, Hootkins—whatever!—dance next week. I couldn't be more pleased. I really couldn't."

I bet, I thought. J.P.'s dad was my father's boss, and my father would like nothing better than to encourage a little dalliance (or is that alliance?) between the two of us, just to cement his own position, of course. But it simply wasn't true and I angrily piped up, "J.P.'s father told you this?"

"Yessiree. We flew back together from the sales meeting and old Ed, well, he had a few too many drinks, got loosened up, and before I knew it, he was telling me about his son's new girlfriend. And that girlfriend was you!"

"He's wrong." I looked away from the disappointment in my father's eyes and glanced helplessly at my mom. But she was offering no support today. She was too busy staring sadly at her ice cream melting behind the centerpiece.

"There is a dance at school next Thursday, the Sadie Hawkins Dance, but I'm not going. Girls have to ask guys, and well, I couldn't do *that.*"

My father frowned at me in bewilderment. "Why the hell not?"

"Because no one would want to go with me, that's why!"

"I just told you Ed Curtin said that J.P. wanted to go with you. What more do you want—an engraved invitation? Just pick up the phone and dial young Curtin. Then you'll have a date for the dance."

"I don't want a date for the dance!" I cried and jumped up. "To this dance or any dance! And if I did, it wouldn't be someone like John Perry Curtin. J.P.'s just a friend. I like talking to him, but— No rockets. No magic. Not like . . ." I let my voice dwindle off as the image of Cal Lindsey sprang into my mind.

"Not like who, baby?" my mother asked softly.

"Cal Lindsey," I whispered, only too happy to say the special name. Did the air in the dining room suddenly stir? Did the soft glow from the lamp on the side table flare imperceptibly? My heart quickened as it always did when I thought of him.

"Lindsey, Lindsey," my father muttered, pulling at his mustache. He frowned and then snapped his fingers. "Of course, quarterback for the Bucs and first-string baseball. I read about him in the paper. Fine athlete. Fine young man."

"Not as fine as our Michael," Margaret inserted. Then she said, "If you like this young man so much, why don't you ask him to the dance? He sounds just perfect."

"That's the whole trouble," I said to Mags. "He is perfect. And that's why I'm sure he's been asked to the dance by every other girl at school."

"Nonsense," the little Pekinese growled. "If you asked him, he'd go. Who else is as sweet, as lovely, as charming and popular as you? Why you're darling, you're pretty, you're smart. . . ." The list of my assets went on and on. I faded out.

They both meant well, the wolf and the Pekinese, but their distorted image of me was too much to take. Suddenly, Margaret's chirpy recital scraped across the blackboard of my nerves and something snapped.

"Will you stop it?" I shouted at my mother. "Just stop it! I'm not darling, pretty, or particularly lovely. I'm fat, Mom. Take a good hard look. Everyone at school thinks so, and that's why the phone never rings for me and guys don't show up at the front door. And Daddy, I can't call J.P. like you want because he and I had a big disagreement today. He doesn't like me very much now, and frankly, I don't blame him. I don't like myself very much, either!"

I grabbed my sundae and the bowl of chips and raced upstairs, slamming the bedroom door on Margaret's wounded little cries and my father's blustery anger. But no one pursued me. My mother rather enjoyed playing the martyr, wallowing happily in her hurt feelings, and my father never expended too much time or energy on what he called female adolescent growing pains.

I sat curled up on the floor in my room and turned on the little TV set. With one eye on the screen and the other fixed lovingly on the ice cream, I was all set for the night. But the heroine in this cornball TV show had a size-3 figure. She walked around a lot in skimpy bathing suits and clinging dresses. The men on the show went wild over her body. I got up and turned off the set, then sank back down and concentrated on doing some heavyweight gorging. I needed *something* to get the bitter taste of tonight out of my mouth.

I woke up Saturday morning determined to perfect the plan. But I could only do so much alone. This job required staunch allies. And of those, I had two. Now if only they'd agree to go all the way with me on this crazy scheme!

I called another emergency meeting of the Ugly Ducklings Anonymous for early Sunday afternoon. Both Beverlee and Sonia grumbled over the phone, but finally consented to attend when I promised Mags would cook brunch. With that taken care of, I could relax the rest of Saturday. It was a beautiful day—clear and crisp with little wisps of clouds playing tag across a tie-dyed sky. Mags was downstairs, watching TV and eating home-baked cookies. I started down the steps to join her, when an alien thought gripped me: This is boring. You always watch television with Margaret on Saturday afternoons. How many times can you enjoy another Doris Day–Rock Hudson comedy? Come on. Do something else. Do something exciting.

Like what? I angrily asked this outspoken other self. You know I don't have any exciting hobbies or interests other than nibbling goodies, watching TV, and babbling to Bev and Sonia about Cal Lindsey!

Don't you? the devilish imp persisted.

W-e-l-l . . . The image of my 35-millimeter Nikon exploded in my mind like a flashcube, and I reluctantly conceded that photography had once been the thing in my impressionable youth. For a while there, I thought myself quite the creative soul as I dashed around our town or San Francisco, a camera slung round my neck, snapping unusual shots of buildings or reflections of trees in the water. But that was years ago, when my brother had gone with me and taught me about photography. Now an impish voice was prompting me to reexamine all this stuff.

I moved back into my bedroom and unearthed the large box that contained my camera and all my equipment. I sat on the bed and gently took the camera from its case, putting it to my eye, adjusting the f-stop and focus. My hands went through the routine instinctively. An old album in the bottom of the box caught my eye and I pulled it out. I opened the pages at random and flipped through my photographs, begrudgingly impressed by my own handiwork.

J.P. was right! the persistent imp cried victoriously. You do have a flair.

Yes, I argued, but what good will it do me to get involved with running all over school, photographing stupid clubs, activities, athletic events—

And the Fall Student Council officers? Cal Lindsey was a chief officer of the student government. Cal Lindsey was senior class president, and if I elected to help out J.P., Cal Lindsey would wind up right in the center of my viewfinder.

He would also crop up in athletic shots and God knows how many other photos. The boy was all over the school. It didn't take me too long to realize the unforeseen advantages of helping J.P. with the photography for the yearbook. It just amazed me that I was dense enough to almost miss the chance of a lifetime . . . and all because of my maniacal absorption in getting even with Cotton Candy.

I slid my camera back into the case and put the box on my dresser. Then I scribbled a brief reminder to myself to buy film and put the note on my mirror. "J.P.," I murmured, "I just hope you never find out the real reason behind my taking this photography position on the yearbook staff."

Sunday I learned three things: one, that my shy brother, Michael, was actually inviting a girl home for Thanksgiving dinner; two, that J.P. quite readily forgave me my brief lapse of sanity over Cal Lindsey and welcomed me to his staff as yearbook photographer; and three, and least surprising, desperate women take desperate chances.

The UDA met at the Marshall mansion for brunch and my projected revenge plot. After a stomach-enlarging repast happily prepared by my mother, we three retired to my room and first tackled the title of the project. Beverlee wanted to name it OD (Operation Drano) because in a symbolic sense, we'd be eating away at a phony popularity symbol. I vetoed OD as being too blatantly cruel and instead suggested VP³: Vendetta of the Pom-Pom Princess. Sonia dismissed the business of the name with an impatient flick of her hand. Her analytical mind was already two steps ahead to the actual content of the plot.

"I hope it's not too crazy, Kel," she warned me, hugging

her long, thin knees to her concave chest. "I don't intend to get detention for a buffoon like Taffy Foster."

"Trust me," I said with a small, yet confident smile that belied all my inner tension. I jumped up, closed the door to my room and pulled out my notebook. Late Saturday evening, after "Creature Features," I had stayed up gluing sheets together to have poster-size battle plans drawn up to show the girls. On the large sheets of paper were marked days and times of events, which girl did what, when and how, and the anticipated end results of the separate offensives. I went through the schedule slowly, with Sonia interrupting to ask about how I was going to finance the plan. I explained that I had saved birthday money from all my relatives. Beverlee remained silent throughout the spiel, a tiny curled ball by the edge of my bed, her small foot tapping. There was a frightened look on her face when I finished, and she said, "Let's just not get caught, all right?"

I grinned at her. "No way. It's foolproof."

"Nothing is foolproof."

There was a moment of tension in the room as Beverlee and Sonia examined the battle plans and then each other. Then Sonia cracked a smile at Bev and nodded her curly dark head at me. "Count me in, Kel. It's time we three did something to stop that little twerp."

"I'm in, too," Beverlee added. There was a sparkle in her eyes.

Like I said, desperate women take desperate chances. Sick and tired of being the Ugly Ducklings at Balboa, powerless and overlooked, we decided to take some action to assert ourselves and make a point. Only we didn't bargain on danger until it was too late to back out.

41

✷ five

I would like to say a word about my Dr. Jekyll/Mr. Hyde transformation.

On Monday morning I swaggered into the portals of Balboa a different person. Outwardly, I still claimed ownership of one slightly rotund, thirty-watt profile that beamed as low as you could get. But inside was another story altogether! I had girded my loins with the *plan;* I was geared to do battle against the Pom-Pom Queen.

I came out of biology third period, feverishly ready to put phase one into operation when J.P. bumped into me. He babbled on about my first *Galleon* staff meeting, but dwindled to a halt when he realized how vacant my eyes were. His narrowed dangerously.

"Hey!" he snapped. "You're not listening to me, Kel. And I think you'd better. That is, if you want to stay staff photographer for the yearbook just a little while. This meeting today is very important. I'm assigning all the photo layouts."

I hurried back to the present tense and inclined my head slightly. " 'Speak!' " I commanded with a regal air. " 'Caesar is turned to hear.' "

J.P. shot me a look of black-belt intensity, then strode off down the hall, mumbling audibly, "Who does she think she is—Princess Di?"

Better than that, I smirked to myself, watching J.P.'s lean body recede into the crush of the hallway. Not Princess Di, but Churchill and Gunga Din, Wonder Woman and Attila the Hun all rolled into one: Power and Vengeance El Supremo. And when Taffy Foster got a dose of my bitter medicine, the Pig Woman would cast away her trough and rise victorious from the mire. Then other people besides me would recognize a Class-A leader and brain. Other people . . . like Cal Lindsey? With an involuntary quickening of my heart, I clasped my secret battle plans inside my skirt pocket and hurried to meet Sonia. The first lunch bell was about to ring. It was time for phase one.

"It's no good, Marshall," Sonia hissed at me outside the door of the Administrative Office. "All outside gifts or messages *have* to be cleared first by Mrs. Malachi. No exceptions."

"There's always an exception, Sonia!" I retorted. I couldn't stop now. Not when every turn in the halls could bring a humiliating scene with Cotton Candy. A plan flickered in the dark recesses of my brain.

"Oh, no," Sonia sighed, shaking her head. "You've thought of something, haven't you! What do you want me to do?"

She had done quite enough already, and I was very grateful. Actually, I was grateful to both my friends. They had accomplished their objectives Friday afternoon by wangling positions in the two key school areas of power: Sonia used her earlier recommendation from Del Maio to slide into the School Community Service program; shy, apologetic Beverlee capitalized on her superlative reading in English class to get the drama teacher's go-ahead for the public address crew. I couldn't believe it, but VP^3 was going like clockwork. Until now, that is.

I thought quickly. "Look, Sonia, quick get me Mrs. Malachi's phone number. I'll explain later."

Sonia looked puzzled, but obediently hurried inside. In only seconds she was back, rolling her expressive eyes and clutching a scrap of paper.

"My heart," she kept murmuring. "My heart."

"I think sixteen's a little too young to be having a heart attack," I snapped and snatched the paper from her trembling fingers. I looked at my watch. The lunch bell was due to ring in about two minutes. That meant I had to move fast. Taffy took an early period lunch. She'd be out of commission for the next thirty minutes or so. Cal Lindsey, however, was in Advanced Creative Composition. I knew all this from following him around in the early part of the year. Now my idolatry was paying off. Sonia watched me, raking her fingers through her tousled dark curls.

"What are you planning to do with Mrs. Malachi's number?"

"Get her out of the picture."

My friend's mouth trembled. "Wha-a-a-t!"

"Will you quit overreacting! I'm not calling up a contract killer to bump her off. I merely intend to call her from a phone booth and get her away from her desk for five minutes. That way, she won't be there to know anything about a mysterious present that comes in. And you, my dear cohort, can log in the gift and deliver it as part of your official responsibility without taking the blame. If anyone asks questions, just say you're new around here and didn't know you had to wait to clear it with Mrs. Malachi. You got that?"

"But what if Cal wants to know where it came from, *who* it came from? What'll I tell him?"

"He won't ask because he'll be too shocked. Besides, you'll only hand it over to Mr. Confrere. You won't even have to look at C.L. Trust me, Sonia, you won't get into any trouble."

Sonia looked at me, anxiety and excitement sharpening her features.

"You sure this will work, Kel? I mean, the whole—plan?"

Roller-coaster fears kept ripping through my stomach, but I merely grinned confidently and waved a casual hand. "No problem. VP^3 is dynamite, the work of an inspired genius! Now, scuttle back inside and prepare to man Malachi's desk. The delivery people promised me they'd bring in the gift at exactly eleven thirty and they'd come directly to Mrs. Malachi in Administration. I'm off to play Clark Kent in a phone booth. If you don't see Mrs. Malachi leave her desk in two minutes, then start to worry. But not before. Now go!"

"But what happens if she doesn't leave in two minutes?"

I kept the phony grin pasted over my own quivering lips. "Then pray, Sonia. Pray. Or better yet, put that brilliant analytical mind to work and improvise. Now get back inside. You have your instructions."

For a minute, I thought my friend was going to salute. But she only sighed "Here goes" and hurried through the twin frosted doors of the office.

I hurried to the main lobby to find the pay phone. I called Mrs. Malachi's number and, with a sinking sensation, I heard the phone ring on and on.

"Answer! Come on and answer!" I kept repeating, checking my watch. It was 11:28. If the delivery people kept their word, I'd have exactly 120 seconds to get Mrs. Malachi away from her desk and as far from the Administrative Office as possible.

"Mrs. Malachi."

Thank God, I breathed.

"Mrs. Malachi?" I started, then lowered and muffled my voice. "You're wanted by Mrs. Noyes in the Advisors' Office. We have a serious problem out there."

If anything could get Mrs. Malachi jumping out of her seat, it was the mention of the assistant principal's secretary, Mrs. Noyes. Mrs. Noyes was an overbearing, sharp-toothed creature with a mossy fringe of hair who literally and figuratively threw her weight around school, especially in administrative matters. All the kids called her Dragon Lady. I suspect half of the teaching staff did, too. I kept my voice to an obscure mumble, hoping Mrs. Malachi would believe I was one of the little frightened counseling aides who worked in the Advisors' Office, but she was too sharp.

"Who is this?" she asked, distrust coloring the silence over the wire.

I looked desperately at my watch, at the seconds escaping, and took a deep breath. Putting my face out of the booth and speaking through the material of my sleeve, I sharpened my voice and threw all caution to the wind. "This is a serious matter," I repeated. "Please come at once."

"Well . . ." Mrs. Malachi still entertained doubts as to the authenticity of the garbled voice dictating angrily to her, but I could tell she was afraid to risk it. She'd better not incur the wrath of the Dragon Lady. "I'll be right there," she said and hung up.

I fell back weakly against the side of the booth. My heart was knocking uncontrollably like a car filled with low-octane gas. But I had done it. Malachi would be swooping out of her office in five seconds, flying on soft-sneakered soles like a bat all the way across the main quad to the outback region housing the Advisors' Office. And when she got there . . . I shuddered to think of the outcome!

I shuddered to think of what my own outcome would be if Sonia didn't keep her head. In approximately forty-five seconds, my friend would be coolly signing for the first outrageous gift we planned to spring on Cal Lindsey. Oh no, it wasn't coming from the UDA, but from a mysterious source with the damaging initials of T.F. It wouldn't take my Sexy Senior very long to figure out his donor. It wouldn't take my Sexy Senior very long to blow his stack over the humiliating nature of the gift. I was counting on that. Cal Lindsey had a private side to his nature despite his obvious natural talents, and I was just betting that he'd deeply resent the blatant attention from Taffy.

We'd see. I crossed my fingers, gave myself a minute more to get my composure back, then slid out of the booth and sprinted down the halls to the Creative Composition room. Even before I got within view of the door to Confrere's class,

47

I could hear the laughter spilling out, rippling in uproarious crescendoes throughout the silent hallways. Oh God, I prayed, sidling nervously closer to the closed door, please let phase one go off all right. I kept my body flattened off to one side and pressed a beady eye cautiously to the small window in the door, then gasped in shock and delight. The gift I had arranged to have delivered to Cal Lindsey was even bigger and sillier than I could have imagined. Mr. Confrere was trying to keep order, but failing miserably. Even he gave up and began chuckling along with everyone else. Only one person was *not* enjoying himself—Cal Lindsey.

He sat with a scowl on his gorgeous features, one hand holding his blond head, a twitch in his square jaw. Tied to his chair and circling his head were the largest, brightest helium balloons I could have ordered. Small valentine hearts were stuck on each balloon; bright satin ribbons held the uncontrollable mass together in a kittenish, rather sickening bow. But far worse than the balloons was the message streaming over them in poster paint and full hideous view: "I'm high on you! Please be my date for the Sadie Hawkins Dance. T.F."

Confrere finally got some order in the room, but not into those jumbo-jet balloons. Every time someone raised a hand, the air currents would start them knocking together, swaying over Cal's embittered face like drunken, oversize tulips. Cal Lindsey looked like he wanted to kill at that moment. I was praying his anger was directed at Taffy Foster. I giggled, then sped off to share my good news with Sonia and Beverlee.

My good mood lasted almost three days. If I had been more cautious, more realistic, I'd have repeated my father's well-worn adage to myself each dizzying morning: "What goes up,

48

must come down." But I wasn't cautious. I wasn't realistic. The situation at school was too wonderful, too Universal–MGM–Avco-Embassy release-like to even entertain a single doubt that things wouldn't always go my way. I was floating on cloud nine. VP^3 was going beautifully. How was I to foresee the ugly monster that lurked at the end of my fairy tale?

And it was a fairy tale. With each humiliating gift that Ugly Ducklings Anonymous bestowed upon Cal Lindsey, we were holding our heads higher and higher. My birthday money was being spent on the best gift possible—revenge. How we loved watching Cal Lindsey's bafflement and increasing irritation whenever something romantic and foolish was sent to him or done to him at school! Each time a new incident occurred, we'd look at one another and try to contain the laughter, barely holding it in when Taffy wafted by. If the Pom-Pom Queen had heard the rumors that were spreading through school about her and her insane attempts to attract Cal Lindsey, she didn't act concerned. And that was fine with me.

Certainly every planned surprise—the flowers, the boxes of candy, the personal poem in the newspaper—was leading up to the final, humiliating horror, scheduled for the Wednesday afternoon Big Game Rally. One morning Beverlee got on the PA system bright and early with the best imitation of Taffy Foster I've ever heard. I had done an unusually creative job in getting Taffy and her friends to the gym for what they assumed was a last-minute cheering practice. So poor misguided Taffy never got to hear her very own personal invitation to Cal to meet at the Center Wall before the rally Wednesday afternoon. Too bad, because Beverlee put all the gusto, all the sexy oomph into her voice that was morally acceptable on prime-time PA airwaves. By the end of her little spiel, Cal was barely able to control himself, and Taffy couldn't understand at first why smirking stares and whispers followed her through the hallway. Lord knows, I didn't want to enlighten the Brontosaurus Brain. I didn't want to come close to her, not until the dazzling denouement. Because of the rally, Balboa scheduled only two periods in the afternoon. And I eagerly waited to look into those pseudo-green contact-lensed eyes of hers and watch them waver in shame and humbleness. Ahhh, I lived for that moment, and until the rally at two thirty, I wasn't functioning as Kelsey Marshall anymore, but a militaristic general with only one goal in mind: victory over Taffy Foster.

When the last-period bell rang that fateful day, I was already shoving papers and books over my arm and racing to the Center Wall. Sonia had pulled the last job on the list. Knowing my friend's thorough nature, I could rest assured the final phase of VP[3] would go over as smoothly as all the others. But that didn't stop me from hastily securing a ringside seat before the entire school assembled for the Big Game Rally. I searched in vain for Sonia as the crowd began to jam the highly popular Center Wall of the landscaped quadrangle, but gave up when the Pom-Pom girls raced out. The six of them wore the blue-and-gold sweater and skirt outfits, but even in uniform, Taffy Foster stood out. There was an aura about her, a mystique of beauty that made you watch her rather than the five other cheerleaders. She did a graceful cartwheel, long hair streaming; a few males in the audience whistled appreciatively. I muttered and scanned the faces restlessly. Where, oh where, was Sonia? And more important, where was Cal Lindsey?

As if on cue, a roar swelled from the kids as Balboa's football team came running out of the Sports Complex to the front of the Wall. My idol, the Blond Bombshell, led the pack. Hypnotized by his body in the tight-fitting uniform, I stared at him until I felt someone jostle my arm.

"Excuse me, but is this body taken?" a sarcastic, but thoroughly familiar voice said in my ear. "Or is it just out to lunch?"

I turned to see John Perry wedge in beside me. Normally, I would have saved him a place at a rally like this. But not today. Not when salvation and divine retribution were close at hand. And looking into his direct brown eyes, I felt slightly uncomfortable. What if he guessed my motivation for pressing so close to the front? What if he *knew* that I was the ringleader behind the whole Lindsey–Foster farce? He followed my eyes back to Cal and shook his head.

"Still drooling over the impossible dream, I take it. Or have you been changing tactics lately and been going in more for full frontal attack?"

I denied his accusation hotly, but turned my gaze away from Cal. J.P. was too damned sensitive, too perceptive. He reminded me of a hunting dog that picks up a scent and races to seek out the quarry, moist nose quivering and furry body intent. Pity the poor victim trying to escape. In this case, me. I didn't like having J.P. so close to me during the last act of the Pig Woman versus the Pom-Pom Queen. This final curtain was one I wanted to savor all alone.

"What do you keep looking around for?" my bloodhound persisted.

"Who's looking for anyone?" I retorted, at the same time catching a glimpse of Sonia at the back of the crowd. She was quietly directing my last and oh-so-spectacular "gift" to Cal Lindsey.

I took a deep breath and watched with mounting anticipation as the "personal gift" advanced boldly to my idol. This was it. The crowning glory in VP³—the ultimate revenge upon Taffy "Plasticene" Foster. *It* just happened to be one of the sexiest female strippers from our town's Peel-O-Gram service: the highly personal Western Union-type message stripped down, so to speak, to the bare essentials! If the woman they sent was typical, I'd bet that no customers ever filed a complaint, except for shortness of breath or heart attack. The woman was unreal, a Raquel Welch look-alike with dyed blonde hair, wearing the tightest slit-skirt I'd ever seen and a fuzzy postage-stamp sweater that looked as if it had been pasted on. The boys in the crowd went primitive as the vision weaved sinuously up to Cal Lindsey and kissed him. Then she half turned to the crowd, but recited in a clear voice to Cal, "Hi, I'm Wanda La Blue; I've got a striptease message for you! This comes from the heart of a secret fan, who wants you to go to the Sadie Hawkins Dance as her sexy man! Love and kisses, Taffy."

The crowd went wild with laughter and cheers. Taffy Foster's head snapped around as if she were auditioning for the little girl's role in *The Exorcist.* Before Cal could get his vocal cords to unlock, Wanda began to twirl suggestively before him, unzipping her slit skirt. The skirt was lowered slowly and sensuously over what appeared to be midnight black lace panties that could have put Frederick's of Hollywood to shame. The crowd roared. I roared. Even Wanda roared—into more specific action, bumping and grinding her erotic way through a removal of the fuzzy top. Before the amazing Day-Glo bra could be peeled off, Mrs. Noyes swept through the screaming masses and put an abrupt stop to further unveilings. Amid frustrated groans from the rebellious mob, Wanda was firmly handed back her clothes and marched off the premises. Thank goodness she had calmly vowed she could not divulge the name of the paying customer!

But I didn't waste a backward glance at her. My attention was on Cal Lindsey, who stood silently apart in a sea of screaming, jeering kids. He didn't say a word, but his eyes—those sexy, cowboy squinting eyes—said it all. He was staring at Taffy Foster, who kept running her hands through her long hair, a sick look on her face.

In a second, Cal strode over to Taffy and literally yanked her away from her Pom-Pom support system. He pulled her right to the very center of the Wall and blocked her chances of running away. The kids' buzzing instantly died down as they saw what was about to take place. Cal Lindsey, Mr. Cool, the oh-so-private paragon of the senior class, was about to blow up. He was going to lose his temper—and everyone wanted to witness that.

But not as much as me. My breathing had quickened in the weird stillness, and I sensed, rather than saw, J.P. staring at me intently. Come on! I mentally cried to Cal. Let her have it! It's about time the Pretty Person got dumped in public. But before Taffy could get her tongue to stop babbling incoherent protestations of innocence, Cal cut through the noise and laughed. He threw back his head and roared. When he finally managed to choke off his laughter, the tension had dissipated. The scene before me was changing, and I didn't like the feeling I was getting right in the pit of my stomach. Cal rested two strong, tanned arms on Taffy's shoulders and said loudly, "Didn't you ask me a question in that stripper's message— something about going to the Sadie Hawkins Dance with you?

Well, I think you deserve an answer right now. You asked me to go, and I'm now formally accepting. I'd be *honored* to go anywhere with a girl who's been so creative in making a guy feel special. So what do you say—do we have a date?''

The frightened look in Taffy's huge eyes changed to brilliant happiness. And then to subtle calculation as she scanned the crowd and found me, hunched over and colorless, in the front row. A smaller, more private smile hovered on her lips as she watched me and squeezed Cal's arm. "It's a date all right. One I wouldn't miss.''

Cal took her hand and swung it high with a delighted grin. The kids laughed and applauded. "True love!" someone cynically shouted, but the cynicism couldn't hide the fact that something disturbing *was* going on between Taffy and Cal. They were staring at each other with such intensity and wonderment that I felt sickened—and depressed. More than depressed. Crushed. My plan had backfired. It had blown up in my face. Not only had I actually managed to bring Cal Lindsey together with Taffy Foster, but I had sold him a totally false image of a creative, warm, gift-giving Venus. And as much as Taffy resembled Venus de Milo (there were vital parts missing from her, too!), she—in no way—was warm, vibrant, and original. I was the inventive, original one, but cruelly, ironically, this last invention turned out to be a cataclysmic disaster.

And there was nothing I could do now to let Cal know who had really masterminded the romance. Oh no, I was sunk, lower than low, 20,000 leagues beneath the sea, while Taffy was riding high, still the golden girl of the school and now, Cal's date for the Thanksgiving dance. And I had done it. Kelsey "Mastermind" Marshall. *Mastermind,* what a laugh. What a stupid, senseless joke. For I had just masterminded myself into bigger trouble than ever before. Hot bitter tears suddenly stung my eyes, and the scene before me blurred. J.P. immediately turned to me, concern evident in his expression, but I couldn't face him. I couldn't face anybody. With a mumbled excuse, I blindly edged out of the crowd and ran from the quadrangle. Taffy's cheerleading yells followed me all the way to the bus stop.

❋ six

My mother cowered near the keyhole.

"Kelsey, baby. John Perry's downstairs."

I kept the pillow bunched up over my ears and refused to answer.

"He says you've got a special job to do today at the game, taking pictures for the yearbook."

Silence.

"I've never seen J.P. look so cute, Kelsey. You should see him, all dressed up in a nice colorful sweater outfit. Baby? Are you listening?" Margaret's wheedling tone turned frightened when I refused to respond. Whatever could be wrong?

To make matters worse, I had locked myself away on a holiday, and Michael was bringing home a real live girl for turkey dinner. This was big news in my family. But I didn't care. I wanted to suffer, and the bright and sunny skies this morning only infuriated me. It was as if the gods cavorting above were rubbing my nose in my unhappiness, maliciously splashing my room with golden beams of sunlight. It should have been raining violently. Then the game would be called off and Taffy wouldn't pirouette and leap acrobatically across Cal Lindsey's vision, cheering every time he made a touchdown.

But this past Monday I had gone to J.P.'s planning meeting for the *Galleon,* and I had promised to cover the big game. Now I was stuck. I moaned softly and hurled the pillow across the room. It thudded against the door, and Margaret rattled the knob nervously.

"Kelsey! Kelsey! Are you all right in there? You haven't fainted from hunger, have you?"

I bit my lip and refrained from answering, but Margaret had hit a nerve. The truth of the matter was—I was starving, bitterly so. My secret candy supply was depleted, and my stomach was rumbling.

"Kelsey, honey. I've got a treat for you. Your favorite kind of doughnuts, the jelly ones with the powdered sugar. Fresh, too. Daddy went specially to Winchell's for them."

Darn her! I could almost taste the doughnut right now, feel the thick, sweet jelly filling oozing sensuously in my mouth. I knew I shouldn't give in to mere mortal hunger, but I couldn't help it. I grimaced and staggered weakly to the door. When I opened it, Mags straightened up with a birdlike cry of triumph and thrust a plate of doughnuts in my greedy hands.

"I'll tell J.P. you'll be ready in ten minutes," she said, eagerly going down the stairs.

I went to the damn game.

I even took two rolls of film at the event. But my heart wasn't in the Nikon, it was fixed on Cal Lindsey. Every time I watched him snap back and run with the ball, I wanted to cry. He was so unbelievably sexy, so unbelievably athletic. OK. Maybe a Ms. Chubbette couldn't have him. But a synthetic, plastic doll like Taffy Foster shouldn't be allowed to have him either. It just wasn't fair. Wasn't fair. Wasn't—FAIR!

"What isn't fair?" J.P. asked quietly by my side, startling me. I must have gotten so carried away by my feelings that I was talking aloud. Now I nervously gulped and put my eye to the viewfinder.

"Life," I said. "Everything."

J.P. gently but firmly pulled the camera away. I instinctively averted my face, but it was too late. J.P. had already glimpsed the pain and hurt in my eyes.

"Does this have anything to do with Cal Lindsey and Taffy Foster?"

"Oh, spare me the sermon!" I interrupted. "I don't want to hear it. Not *now*, J.P. You just don't understand what I'm going through. You don't know what it's like to be crazy about somebody who doesn't even notice you! Who obviously likes somebody else!"

At that precise moment Cal Lindsey got up from the bench and walked directly up to Taffy Foster. He said something low to her and ran his finger along her cheek. Taffy seemed to melt. The Barbie doll actually seemed to melt and simper back at him, and in seconds, they were both leaning close together and smiling over a private joke.

A giant hand reached into my body, seized my heart and gripped it hard. I couldn't take it. I just couldn't take it. My stupid plan had blown up in my face—the man of my fantasies was falling for the girl of my nightmares.

Then, two animated girls brushed past us babbling about the Sadie Hawkins Dance.

"Bringing Todd, Amy?" the shorter, dark-haired girl asked, stopping right behind us.

Amy, a pretty, curly-haired blonde, shook her head and for some strange reason, glanced directly at John Perry.

"No, ah, I, ah, wanted to ask somebody else."

Now was I crazy or did the girl's friend stare directly at J.P. too? She giggled and mumbled, "You'd better hurry up then and do it. The dance is tonight, you know!"

"I know," little Amy said.

J.P. looked over at her and grinned, waving a hand in casual greeting. "Hi, Amy."

Was she actually blushing at J.P.'s greeting? Was I really here, or in The Twilight Zone? I couldn't get over the fact that I had somehow stumbled into a foreign movie, and everyone was speaking a different language.

Amy gazed adoringly at J.P., screwed up her courage and suddenly blurted, "Um, J.P.? Uh, I was wondering. That is, uh, if no one's asked you, well—" She stopped, fear holding her back from making the plunge. How well I could identify with that fear! Her aggressive friend poked her in the ribs, and Amy said in tape recorder fast forward, "Well, um, I wondered if you'd go to the Sadie Hawkins Dance with me?"

She stood there, a miserable tangle of knots and hopes. Not a bad-looking girl, at all. In fact, if I were to be perfectly honest, quite a pretty girl—a little young, but with a good figure. And here she was, holding her heart out to cool, emotionless John Perry Curtin. I was shocked. Stunned. I never figured *any* girl interested J.P. Or vice versa. He was simply too busy at school with his yearbook and his sports to get all hot and bothered with the female gender. Well, well, well. The sly fox. The old dog.

He didn't act like one, however. To give him credit, he simply thanked Amy, but told her he would be going to the dance in an official capacity for the yearbook. "Oh" was what the girl said. But, as she turned and walked away with her friend, the disappointed droop to her mouth said much much more.

"Listen, Kelsey," he smiled suddenly, reaching over to squeeze my arm. "I've got a good idea. Why don't we *both* go to the dance this evening? Uh, I mean, in a strictly professional capacity," he hastily amended, catching my raised eyebrows. "You could take some shots of the event, and I could take notes. What do you say? Are we a team?"

There was an unfathomable light in J.P.'s eyes. For just a minute he seemed vulnerable, nervous. Moments before that he had been a love object to some infatuated little freshman or sophomore. It was all too strange to me. *The Three Faces of Eve* had nothing on John Perry Curtin. I decided I didn't know him quite as well as I thought I did, but then the picture righted itself. "Are we a team?" he asked. *A team.* The most unromantic images sprang to mind: a team of horses dragging a wagon, a team of oxen plowing the soil, a football team working precisely together for a common good. Football. My heart yanked back to the painful scene of the quarterback flirting with the cheerleader. My vision blurred and I thrust the camera to my eyes quickly. "Yeah, we're a team, J.P.," I muttered in a colorless tone. "You'll see me at the dance."

But I never made it.

60

I suffered a mini-breakdown during Thanksgiving dinner at our house and fled upstairs before my second helping of pumpkin pie. I think my brother precipitated the breakdown. My brother's reaction to his girlfriend, that is. He was so obviously crazy about her, so attuned to her every little wish and command. The looks he kept giving her all through the meal were devotion-filled, calflike, *obsessed*. Just the kind of looks I wanted from Cal Lindsey, looks which he'd probably never give me. Yet glancing covertly at Mike's girl, Priska Rodgers, I couldn't understand the attraction at all! I mean, here was my tall, good-looking older brother, a trifle shy, a football star, a photography nut, drooling over this quiet, tiny mouse of a girl. Priska did have lively gray eyes with dark lashes, but otherwise all around standard-ration features. She was plain, for pete's sake. So-so. Ho-hum. Even her simple blouse and camel slacks seemed prepackaged and lackluster. I wouldn't mind if Priska's body was dynamite. That might partially explain her hold on my brother. But when she took off her light jacket, there was nothing to write home about there, either. I couldn't understand it. Yet Michael leaned toward her every word. Laughed at her little attempts at humor. Jumped up and did her bidding without an embarrassed air. You'd think Princess Leia had blown in from *Star Wars*.

I could take only so much before my stomach started twisting and my brain replayed torturous scenes from the morning. I threw out an excuse to the startled group around the table and hurried upstairs. Halfway to my room I heard Mags come squeaking after me, but then my father's brusque voice stopped her. Good for ole grumpy Dad, I thought. If there was one person I couldn't talk to at this point, it was my mother. She would only sidle nervously around the room, throwing out indecisive questions and trying to placate me with food.

Well, food could not alter this lousy situation. I took a good hard look in the mirror at my porcine little cheeks and puffball body and flung myself dramatically on the bed. In doing this, I knocked over my diary, which rested on the small nightstand. All the photographs of Cal Lindsey that I had clipped from the school paper came tumbling out of the book, visions of his beautiful face and body flew up in the air and came to land tantalizingly close to me on the bed.

Great sobs choked my throat, and I fell back against the bed. I don't think I ever felt as lonely or as desolate before in my entire life. I knew I could call either Sonia or Beverlee, but I was too embarrassed. After the fiasco yesterday, I was ashamed to admit to them how terribly sorry I was to have ensnared them in such an ill-fated plot. And J.P.? My old faithful friend and confidante? I shuddered to think of the reaction I'd get from him once I made a clean confession of my sins.

Niagara Falls was threatening to overflow again. I had just stumbled off the bed to get a box of tissues when I heard a tentative knock on my door. Before I could yell "Go away!" the door opened and Michael's girlfriend, Priska, poked her head in.

"Hi," she said softly. "I was coming up here to comb my hair, and I heard you crying in here. Is there anything I can do to help? I'm good at problem solving. It's my minor in college."

For a second I was too stunned to do anything. Then "No, no," I said, wiping the tears away with a rough swipe of my hand. "I'm fine, really."

And I weigh ninety pounds.

And Cal Lindsey has just seen the light and realizes he adores me.

And I'm the biggest liar this side of Kenwood Avenue.

When Priska said again with genuine interest, "Tell me about it," I did. I opened my mouth and became Chatty Cathy. I burbled on for nearly half an hour about my feelings for Cal Lindsey and the horrific fiasco I caused. I don't know what Priska possessed, but it was magical enough to pull the whole uncut, unedited story from me. At the end of the recital, I felt less grief-stricken. I raised grateful eyes to this strange girl, but she was off, lost in her own thoughts.

"You know what you need?" she said suddenly, jerking back to face me. "You need MMGs."

"MMGs? What are those?" I asked.

She grinned at me. "Magic Male Grabbers. Tips to attract guys. Why do you think your brother is so crazy about me? Sheer chance or luck? No way. The whole romance was conceived and plotted from the word *go*. And all I used was MMG."

MMG. I seized upon the three letters like Sir Galahad discovering the Holy Grail. "You really believe I could get some guy to like me, using these tricks?"

"Like you? Try adore you! Try love you. And not any guy. Shoot for the one you want: Cal Lindsey."

"Oh, no, I couldn't. I—he—well, he's in a different class than me, he wouldn't give me a second look. . . ."

Priska frowned. I found my voice dwindling under her displeasure. Suddenly I realized the magnetism she must exert upon my brother. Her belief in herself, and in her Magic Male Grabbers, was awesome. And just a little frightening.

"Not only will Cal Lindsey give you second looks, he'll

drop this Taffy Foster character so fast her empty head will swim. Trust me. This is the way to go."

When I discovered what the "way" entailed, I wasn't quite as gung ho about MMG as before. Basically, the tricks were part reverse psychology, part *Cosmopolitan* magazine, a dash of winning through intimidation, and a dose of just plain out-and-out deviousness, lies, and game playing. I heard Priska out, marveling at her brazenness while at the same time disliking the fact that she was so blatantly manipulating my brother and other people around her. Yet it seemed to work so well with Michael. And was it truly hurting Michael if he seemed so happy?

"Well, what do you think? Want to give it a go?" Priska smiled at me. I scratched my head and frowned. As much as I worried about Cal Lindsey and Taffy Foster, I didn't believe at this time that their romance would develop into anything except one unpleasant outing together. I just knew my idol would have the good sense to uncover the Pom-Pom Queen's true ugly nature at the end of the evening and would dump her without a moment's hesitation. In fact, the more I thought about it, the better I felt. Why hadn't I seen the light before?

So I grinned now at Priska Rodgers and her Magic Male Grabbers and filed them away under Funny Ideas. I'm glad I'm such a methodical person, because the very next morning I learned something so horrifying that it sent me racing to those exact same mental file cabinets to pull them out again!

❋ seven

I hate hero sandwiches.

To this day I can't pick one up without associating bad news with it. Like the news I overheard at the New York Deli the very next afternoon. The Deli is Balboa's local hangout, a casual, scruffy off-the-wall delicatessen that caters to big appetites. And to kids who want to sit in the back and talk for hours, as well as stuff their faces. It was a perfect place to unwind on a Friday afternoon or to exchange the latest gossip about who was cheating on whom. Romances were conceived and ended there, homework was stealthily copied, and fights cooled off.

And once, to my own personal knowledge, a heart was broken there. And I should know. It was my own heart.

But I hadn't started out that slightly cool, overcast Friday morning in a blue mood. If anything, the weather was in direct contrast to my spirits. While the sky outside my window was cold slate gray, the atmosphere inside my bedroom was sunny, with a warming optimistic trend. After the talk with Priska the night before, I felt confident that the Lindsey–Foster alliance was already an obsolete one. In fact, I mused gaily, Taffy might very well be sulking in her own bedroom right now, a pout putting tiny creases in that perfectly creamy complexion. Ha! As I whirled around the room getting dressed, I took time to dial J.P. to see if he would forgive me for failing to show at the dance last night. His younger sister, Ruth Anne, answered and told me her lazybones brother was still pounding the pillow. I decided not to bother him and hung up. Then I called Sonia and Beverlee and invited them to go for submarine sandwiches at the Deli—my treat. It was my way of telling them how sorry I was about VP³. Their eagerness to get together touched me, and I realized what a valuable possession I had in their friendship.

Things were looking up all right. Except on my bathroom scale. There I was pleased to note that things were looking down. I had actually lost two full pounds over this last hectic week. Maybe all the trauma and angst over being in love was a sensational new way to diet! Whatever the cause, I hoped I could keep on doing it. It would be so wonderful to be able to select jeans and shirts from the low numbers on the rack.

I tucked all these positive thoughts inside my head. Then I bounced out of the house with a cheery good-bye to my family who were lazing around the patio, searching in vain for the sun. Priska slanted a small private glance at me that contained a question in it. I grinned back in answer and raced out the door. Nothing against my brother's girlfriend, but who needed to manipulate people like mindless robots when life was so wonderful?

I did, it seemed, not more than fifteen minutes later when the three of us were happily ensconced in the largest back booth of the Deli, the one with the really private partition. In front of our eager faces were the largest, juiciest concoctions we'd ever seen. Paolo, the "chef," had really outdone himself this time. Sonia moaned and poked at her sandwich before picking it up. "How can I—how can *we*—be sick enough to jam all these calories down our throats when we stuffed ourselves yesterday!"

"Relax," I retorted with a grin. "We probably burned them all off just by trotting over here."

"Sort of like advanced premature exercising?"

"Something like that," I giggled, and took the first plunge. And stopped, midbite, when I overheard a remark from the five kids sitting in the adjacent booth. I hadn't been paying too much attention to their conversation, which primarily dealt with how they spent their holiday and if they got to go to the big game. But the mention of a familiar name snagged my total attention.

"I didn't know J.P. Curtin and Amy Lanier were such a hot item," someone was saying. "But you should have seen them together last night at the dance. If he danced any closer to her, she could have used him for wallpaper. Geez! It was obscene!"

One of the girls whispered something else and everyone broke up. I broke up, too, but not in laughter. In shock. I don't remember putting my hero sandwich down or automatically reaching for my diet soda. In between tasteless sips, I could see Beverlee's eyes seeking Sonia's with concern.

"Stupid kids," Sonia hissed. "They're only joking, Kelsey.

67

Blowing something minor way out of proportion. I'm sure of it. You know John Perry. Can you see him swooning all over a girl? I can't. He's just not like that."

"Yeah," Beverlee hurriedly chimed in. "You know he never gets involved with anybody. You're the only girl he really likes."

"As a *friend*, you mean," I said. "You know there's nothing between the two of us. There never has been. And there never will be."

"Kelsey, it's OK." Sonia shook her head. But I was too wound up, too stunned to stop. Somehow the image of John Perry Curtin dancing slowly and intimately with that pretty girl Amy threw me. It threw me so much, I couldn't understand my emotions. What was happening to me? I was obsessed with Cal Lindsey, wasn't I? Not good old J.P. Curtin. Cal Lindsey got my pulses racing, and my heartbeat thumping. So why was I acting like the final earthquake had hit Crestwood Heights and my world was shifting its axis? It certainly couldn't be jealousy over the fact that a friend of mine had normal feelings about a girl who so obviously adored him. Since it couldn't be jealousy, it must be another emotion—like anger. Yes, that's it. I must be furious because J.P. lied to me when he told me yesterday he was going to the dance in a professional capacity for the *Galleon*. And J.P. never lied to me. It was part of what made him, us, our friendship, so special.

I summoned up a laugh. "Hey, come on, everybody! No one's died. This isn't a wake, or the end of the world. I'm *glad* J.P.'s finally found himself a girlfriend. Really I am. Now he'll stop bugging me on Saturday nights to join him for dinner or a movie. Really, this is—great."

The last word cracked slightly, but I had to admit I was

pretty convincing. I convinced myself. Only Sonia and Beverlee looked doubtfully at each other. I settled back to enjoy my sandwich, but found I was much happier when I ordered the biggest, gobbiest sundae on the menu for dessert. To hell with the new diet. *Carpe diem*—seize the day—and all that. I waved a particularly gooey spoonful of chocolate fudge ice cream at my friends in a mock toast. "Here's to friendship!" I cried.

"To friendship," Sonia and Beverlee repeated, but the festive atmosphere in which we had originally sat down had fled. Everyone ate quickly and we left the Deli feeling strained. It was my fault really for keeping up such a forced fun facade. The facade cracked even more two blocks from the intersection in town. With a roar and a flash of color, a bright red sports car came hurtling to a stop alongside us.

"Say, isn't that . . . !"

I simply nodded, too choked up to respond properly to Sonia's unfinished question. It was Cal Lindsey's Triumph and Cal Lindsey's head that leaned out the window at us. "Hi," he said, with that marvelous grin. His macho tinted sunglasses hid those sexy eyes, but they made him look even harder, even tougher. A girl could be accused of mental molestation just by staring into that face. Since no one thought to reply, I stammered out an inane and weak-sounding hello.

"Listen, you're Kelsey Marshall, aren't you? J.P. Curtin told me you're the person I should talk to about the football pictures from yesterday's game—"

"You were wonderful," I dreamily interrupted. "Fantastic. Those touchdowns at the end of the third quarter saved the game for us."

He waved a dismissing hand as if he had heard it all before. Probably he had. It was then that I spotted his passenger— Taffy Foster! She sat smugly, contentedly, in the little bucket seat, a vision (nightmare!) in a cream-colored sweater and matching beige cord jeans. My astonished eyes met hers, and I swear she winked at me. A condescending, oh-so-contemptuous lowering of the eyelid. "Ha, ha," it seemed to say. "We have our little secret, don't we?"

Cal noticed the subtle signs of recognition and politely said, "Oh, do you two know each other," but Taffy stopped him with a simper. And then did something I couldn't believe was possible. She started coughing, but interspersed with the hacking noises were the unmistakable sounds of a pig! Instantly, my face flamed bright red and my adrenaline started flowing. How dare she? How could she! I'd die if Cal realized what she was doing. With a furious, barely controlled grimace at her, I masked my anger and turned my attention to what Cal Lindsey was saying. He was asking me about developing the prints so he could get some good ones made up for Coach Griggs as a gift from the team.

"So when do you think you'll have them ready?"

"Ready?"

"The prints of the game Thursday."

His tone was patient and kind, but I felt like a backward child, unable to remember anything beyond the simplest things. I couldn't concentrate, not with this hot fury burning my gut, not with my arch rival staring at me intently, pityingly.

"Oh, uh, the prints. Sure. I can get them done Monday during lunch. How's that? You can stop by the *Galleon* staff office to check them out any time after one."

"Great!" He patted the edge of the car happily like a baby who's been handed a great colorful rattle. I wanted to pick him up and squeeze him to death. I wanted to do more than change his diapers, however. Those dimples were too much.

"J.P. said you were good. I believe it. This means a lot to

70

me, Kelsey. Thanks. I'll check back with you on Monday."
And with a gunning of the engine and a quick wave he was
off, hurtling down the street. I could see Cotton Candy's head
lean close to his as they turned a corner. If I were into primal
screaming, I'd have thrown back my head and let all the anger,
pain, and frustration come out in one great roar. But we were
walking into the oh-so-proper burg of Crestwood Heights.
Happily adjusted adolescents of Crestwood Heights don't
stand in the middle of town beating on their chests like enraged gorillas.

So I did the only other thing open to me.

I sold my soul to the devil and apprenticed myself to Priska
Rodgers. Oh, I knew the dangers involved in learning Magic
Male Grabbers, but I didn't care at that point. I needed something drastic to counterbalance my overriding feeling of pow-
erlessness and hurt. I told myself I needed to use MMG for
Cal Lindsey, as revenge against Taffy Foster. But in the back
of my mind a small inner voice was whispering, And what
about John Perry Curtin?

For the remainder of Friday afternoon, I followed my
brother's girlfriend around the house, scribbling down every
sneaky, conniving tip and rule she threw my way. By the end
of the day my little black notebook was crammed to bursting
with some potent material. The Sorcerer's Apprentice, who
suddenly discovers the gift of the Master. Only I prayed that
unlike the Disney cartoon character of the same name, I
wouldn't let my brand of magic zoom out of control. That was
the whole point. Control . . . and Cal Lindsey. I sighed with
excitation over that grouping.

At the end of the "lesson," Priska invited me to do a tour
of the Stanford Shopping Mall. She still seemed all fired up to
continue babbling about MMG, but I recognized the fact that

my brother had invited this girl to stay at our house for the weekend. Not me. And so far, he hadn't seen her at all today since early afternoon.

"But Priska, but, ah, Michael . . ." I stuttered. "I mean, what will my brother say about your going out on a Friday night with *me*? Won't he be furious?"

The little gray-eyed mouse delicately swung her foot along the side of my bed. A faint smile touched her lips, then disappeared so fast I couldn't swear it had been there in the first place.

"Your brother will be all too happy to drive us there after dinner and wait for us at the Mall until we're finished."

"But Mike hates shopping. He loathes the Mall!"

"He likes it now," she coolly said. "Because *I* like it. And he does what I like. C'mon. We have to finish MMG properly and get you a brand-new image. A physical one, I mean."

What could I say?

I said yes. Despite subtle signs of displeasure, my brother said yes, too, confirming to me how effective Priska's tricks really were. After dinner, we three trooped all through the Mall through department stores and boutiques like the Three Wise Men dying to find just the perfect gift for the newborn child. Only, in this case, I was the baby they were shopping for. With amazing fashion sense and surety, Priska had me charging a whole ensemble of colorful tops, pants, and dresses. Thank God for Margaret's generosity and her credit cards! Then Priska walked me over to Supercuts and personally supervised the styling of a new hairdo: a daring, short, layered look, cropped jaggedly, wickedly close to my head like a sleek cap. Quite the change from chin-length, straight hair! We finally found ourselves at a cosmetic counter in

Macy's, and guess who was in the makeup seat, buying eye shadows and blushers right and left? You guessed it.

By the time we finished the Magical Mystery Tour, I was a completely changed person. Outwardly, that is. Externally, I looked slimmer, more fashionable—prettier? My hair actually gave my cherubic cheeks the illusion of cheekbones, while my smoky plum and gray eye shadows highlighted my hazel eyes. Priska stood off to one side, Professor Henry Higgins to my Eliza Doolittle, confidently eyeing the transformation. But my brother really boosted my sagging morale. "God, Kelsey!" he exclaimed, twirling me around. "You look fantastic!"

Maybe that's how I *looked*.

How I felt was another matter entirely.

Despite the thorough and amazing make-over, I still envisioned myself as Baby Bloated, waddling through the front door of 24 Kenwood Avenue to my parents' incredulous stares. I still felt cocooned in subcutaneous fat, even though my dad rushed to get his camera to take pictures of me. Internally, I was still smarting from my wounds. I had gone through one of the roughest twenty-four hours of my life, and a little cosmetic camouflage wasn't about to solve all my problems. But it helped. Oh yes, it helped.

What made me feel even more optimistic was the phone call I received from John Perry. He called just as my dad was snapping my picture by the fireplace so my mother only said, "Just a minute, J.P." and left him dangling. I started walking eagerly to the phone when Priska shot out a restraining arm and blocked my way.

"Oh no you don't," she hissed. "You're not home right now."

"But, it's J.P., Priska. A—a *friend*. I'm always home to J.P."

73

"That's exactly my point," she retorted. "MMG #6: Never be predictable. Don't be in one spot all the time. Be out sometimes. Be more mysterious about your activities."

"But . . . I have to talk to J.P. now. I have to apologize for not showing at the dance last night and—"

"You mean the dance where people spotted this guy putting the moves on another girl?"

That stopped me. I had confided all this to Priska, and now the hurt and jealousy rose up in my throat and I finally saw the light. Why was I always the one to apologize first? Why was I always home when he called or around when he needed my help? He certainly didn't need my help last night!

I waved to Margaret to return to the phone.

"I'm out," I mouthed silently to her. "On a date. Period."

She repeated my words to J.P. I heard a faint squawking noise at his end of the phone, and then Margaret hung up. There was a puzzled expression on her face.

"What? What is it?" I eagerly demanded.

"I'm not sure," my mom frowned. "I've never heard John Perry sound so, well, abrupt. Disturbed. It's not like him. He insisted that you call him back the minute you get home tonight."

Priska caught my eye and smiled in a knowing way. She came close to me and whispered, "Jealous, most likely. Probably annoyed as anything because his security blanket is pulling the rug out from under his feet."

A feeling of elation warred with common decency and courtesy. "But shouldn't I call him back later . . . tomorrow morning? I still want to explain to him why I didn't go to the dance."

But Priska shook her head vigorously. "Never explain *anything*. You don't have to. And don't call him back like he orders. No. Be hard to reach the rest of this weekend. Make him wonder what you're doing, and who with. Men need their leashes tightened every so often. I think it's time J.P. got his pulled."

I've thought of J.P. Curtin in many ways, but never as a wayward puppy. And somehow Cal Lindsey did not fit the bill as a German shepherd or a collie. But if becoming a successful devotee to Magic Male Grabbers meant thinking of men as such, then Great Dane! I'd do it. I nodded at Priska and soared up the stairs to my room, all too eager to tell Sonia and Beverlee about my magic make-over. But not all of the make-over. Not the part about MMG. Not just yet. After I had snagged the Sex Machine as mine, then maybe. But not just yet.

✳ eight

MAGIC MALE GRABBER #1: You're the prettiest girl at school. Even if you're not, believe you are. This attitude alone will make you appear more attractive.

MAGIC MALE GRABBER #2: Walk confidently, with purpose, wherever you go. Hold your head up and your shoulders back.

MAGIC MALE GRABBER #3: Make eye contact with all kinds of people. Smile at them once you've got their attention.

MAGIC MALE GRABBER #4: Keep a little smile on your face at all other times as well. A private smile suggests a sense of confidence in yourself or a delicious secret you're hiding. Either effect is good to cultivate. Work at it!

MAGIC MALE GRABBER #5: Always accept a compliment

gracefully. Never shrug it off or belittle yourself when somebody says something good about you. Act as if you believe it. Smile and simply say, "Thank you."

MAGIC MALE GRABBER #6: Never be predictable. Don't be in one spot all the time. Be out sometimes. Be more mysterious about your activities.

There were over fifty of these MMGs crammed in my little black notebook, but somehow I had gotten stuck reading and rereading only the first six. Because they were the least action-oriented and therefore nonthreatening? Possibly. Or maybe because they seemed to apply so directly to my condition on the first day back at school. Dressed in a racy magenta jumpsuit with cute rope sandals and cloisonné necklace that Priska had selected, and made up as I had been taught, I had never received so many stares or compliments. Don't get me wrong. I was not (suddenly) the belle of the ball, a femme fatale. (Fat fatale was still how I saw myself!) But I did look markedly different, and as the UDA kept kidding me, my low-profile days were over.

I had just gotten used to reacting to kids' astonished stares and nice comments when I got thrown a curveball. And wouldn't you know that John Perry Curtin was the pitcher! I was finishing up in the darkroom of Mr. Willins' lab; he teaches photography at school and lets the *Galleon* staff as well as the newspaper people develop prints in his darkroom. The two rolls of film from the game on Thursday had turned out nicely. Not as professional as my usual quality, but then I had other things on my mind that gloom-ridden morning. I was just hanging the best shots to dry so Cal Lindsey could review them easily when I heard a tentative knock on the door.

"Come in," I called loudly. "The red light's off."

I had my back to the door so I didn't see who had entered until I turned around. And then I felt slightly foolish and tongue-tied. It was J.P., but he didn't say anything to me. He just stood there with an odd expression on his normally smiling, good-natured face.

"Why, whatever's the matter with you?" I tried to joke, forcing a hollow laugh, when the silence lengthened between us. He just kept standing there, staring at me.

"What happened to *you*?" he finally got out.

Oh, I thought. Of course. He's shocked by my transformation and probably is thinking of a way to compliment me. I was all set to practice MMG #5 one more time as I coyly reached up to arrange my hair. "You mean this—and all this?" I giggled, waggling an encompassing hand at my outfit and face.

"No," he snapped with some heat. "I can see the changes myself. I mean your absence at the Sadie Hawkins Dance and the fact that you never called me back all weekend. I told your mother it was urgent that you return my call that same evening. That was Friday night. I didn't hear from you later that evening or all day Saturday or Sunday. What happened to you, Kelsey?"

I could see how upset he was, and I started to think up a good dramatic story to feed him when Priska's cool voice sounded in my mind, *Never explain. You don't have to. If J.P. is upset, so be it.*

"I was—out," I calmly said, and turned back to the prints. "I got home too late to call you."

"And Saturday and Sunday?"

"Busy." The one-word answer came out too brusquely, and I quickly hunched over the chemical tray.

"Busy," J.P. repeated behind me. "Busy the entire three days? I don't believe you. What were you doing?" His usually calm, collected voice rose several octaves, and I wheeled to face him, almost enjoying the spectacle of seeing Cucumber Curtin lose his control. "Men need their leashes tightened," Priska had said. All the rest would naturally follow. Here was a perfect case in point. Perfect until J.P. shattered my smug illusion.

"Frankly, Kelsey, I don't care what you do. Or who you do it with. That's your business. But when it involves me, it becomes my business. I asked you to the dance on Thursday night because I needed a photographer. Did you think it was just a joke? I don't joke about the *Galleon* or its deadlines. You should know that better than most people. I had a hard time finding a replacement for you that night—"

"What about Amy Lanier?" I interrupted. "Wasn't she an acceptable replacement?" I was too stung to realize what I was saying. I must have broken about sixteen MMGs when I mentioned her name in such an emotional way, but I wasn't thinking about Magic Male Grabbers and control at that moment. I was thinking about John Perry Curtin and me.

"Amy Lanier?" J.P. spit the name out in angry puzzlement. "What the hell does she have to do with this?"

"Nothing!" I screamed. "Everything!"

I was losing control of the situation when a new expression on J.P.'s face instantly turned me around. His anger and confusion melted into a tiny personal smile, as if he were experiencing the sensation of little Amy swooning into his arms on instant replay. I gritted my teeth. I hardened my heart.

"Look, Kelsey, why don't we talk about that?" J.P. offered, taking a step closer to me. "If you've heard something, and

79

it's bothered you, let's get it out in the open." Although his warm, chocolate-brown eyes melted to Hershey sweetness behind the wire rims, I wasn't taken in. Oh, the smug little devil. To think I nearly played right into his two-timing hands. I blessed the day I learned about Magic Male Grabbers because an appropriate bit of advice sprang instantly to mind: "Avoid getting too personal in matters of the heart. If the boy in question wants to zero in too directly on your feelings, don't let him. Be light and casual. This will keep him off-balance and let you maintain the upper hand in the relationship." So I downshifted from fourth to neutral and gently, casually, laughed.

"I'm not bothered, J.P. Not at all. I was kidding you before about Amy Lanier, and you fell for it! Why ever should it disturb me if you enjoy yourself at a dance? That's all I heard and frankly, I think it's marvelous."

His features distinctly sagged. "You do?"

"Yes," I coolly assured him. "I do. And after all, I was out myself, having a good time. I guess that's why I never did return your call. I was so busy the message flew right out of my mind, and I forgot the rest of the weekend. I'm really sorry you were stuck at the Sadie Hawkins Dance. Really, I am."

I finished hanging the last print and rustled by him briskly.

"So, are we still close friends, J.P.?" I asked, rubbing salt in the wounds. "I mean, close friends don't have to have full-length explanations for something perfectly normal, do they? Let's leave it at that, OK?" And with that, I pushed past him into the hallway. He looked at me strangely, with a question in his eyes, but I didn't take the time to enlighten him. I was too anxious to move away from the emotional little scene. I sensed I had scored a point, but I felt disturbed.

Practically everything I had told J.P. had been lies, and I wasn't used to being dishonest with him. It bothered me immensely about Amy Lanier, and I wanted nothing more than to hear John Perry out about this sticky issue. But MMG told me that wasn't in the cards. Not if I wanted to keep the power position with guys. I pulled out the little black notebook absently and frowned at it. Would I always feel so, well, strange about using these tricks to keep control of situations? Would it always seem unnatural to lie so blatantly to someone I liked so much?

I got my answer on Friday.

The whole purpose of Magic Male Grabbers was to attract Cal Lindsey and woo him away from the Taffy-Pull Princess. So far, I had been wading in the baby end of the pool, testing the method on smaller fish before plunging in the deep end. Originally I may have hated baiting my hooks with such out-and-out lies, but the amount of trusting little fishes I yanked in dispelled my early qualms and stabs of conscience.

Two smaller fish who changed my wallflower image were Danny Ortiz and Steve Nelson, friends of Cal Lindsey's and fellow football jocks. MMG #15 told me: "Moving up to a different level can seem intimidating, but it isn't really. Not if you manage to befriend a fringe person of the crowd you want to infiltrate. Acceptance is merely a trick of appearance." In other words, get in with Cal's friends as subtly as you can, and you get close to the GOLD.

I chose my two targets carefully. Besides the obvious reason of being good buddies with my idol, the two athletes were also somewhat vain and status-conscious. What better way to snare their attention than by using my position as yearbook photographer? Using stolen letterhead from the Administrative Office (thanks to Sonia again), I invited them to pose for a special sports section for the *Galleon*. The communication, an official-sounding paper from Mr. Del Maio's own desk, advised them to cooperate gracefully and to keep the assignment quiet. "The photographer in question will be Kelsey Marshall," the letter stated. "Please contact her for a session this coming Friday."

Oh, I loved the reactions I got from classmates and friends when the two superhunks cornered me separately in public. Danny "The Force" Ortiz and Steve "Exterminator" Nelson actually picking the little Pig Woman out of a crowd to laugh and talk intimately with her? Or so it seemed to the shocked grapevine, that constantly throbbing pulsebeat of hotbed lust and gossip at the heart of Balboa High. Is it true? Rumors began circulating. Has The Force Ortiz, with his Latin smoldering eyes and dark curly hair, got a secret yen for Kelsey Marshall? And what about the Buccaneers' top linebacker: Was Exterminator getting what appeared to be a phone number from the aforementioned mystery woman? The back booths of the New York Deli pounded in true primitive jungle-beat rhythm . . . the bathrooms at school, the other focal (vocal?) points of intrigue resounded with hushed, incredulous questions. How did it feel to be on the other side of *The National Enquirer*: the gossip*ee* rather than the gossip*er*?

I loved it. Really loved it. My hitherto nonexistent romance rating at school shot up points when I casually made dates with both Danny and Steve. Of course, I told no one that these hot and heavy assignations were only times for a photo shooting, Danny's at lunchtime and Steve's right after school on Friday afternoon.

In the very beginning, I hated lying to John Perry. But as the week wore on, I minded it less and less. Until on Friday, at lunchtime, I actually started to enjoy it. And that's when I should have pulled back in horror and given myself a great hard shake. Being dishonest to such a King Krumb as J.P. Curtin was turning out to be was not very hard. We had stopped communicating after the scene in the darkroom, which was fine with me. But being deliberately dishonest to my family and my friends was quite a strain. I thought I could swing it as easily as Priska could, leading my poor deluded brother by a ring in his nose, but I couldn't. Half of the fun in being the Creature from the Blob Lagoon from before MMG was the freedom I had to spill my guts to Sonia and Beverlee. If they asked me why I looked so down, I could grumble and then discuss the whole issue until it was resolved. I could be *me*. Just me. And act as naturally as I wanted.

Now I found myself relating to my two close friends like I was blocked up behind the Great Wall of China. "Is it true, Kel?" they'd squeal at me, after watching Dan the Man amble away with a cool "Catch ya later." "Is it true Ortiz asked you *out*?"

I simply stood there and shrugged with an enigmatic smile.

"But tell us!" Sonia would persist, all excited and animated over my great good fortune. And I would act like the Empress of the Ming Dynasty, sending back an order of roast duck with an imperious, blank stare. "There's nothing to tell," I'd say, watching their faces droop. "Really."

After a while, both my friends stopped asking. And I could stop lying to them. Of course, there was a lot to tell. But I vowed I wouldn't make a fool of myself by spilling it all out until I saw some results. So, as lonely as I felt, I kept the UDA on the outskirts of my new life-style and welcomed some new faces in.

There was Harry Franco from French, with the dirty blond hair and perennial beret, and Burt Liu in homeroom and Jim Orr from the *Galleon* staff and . . . but I could go on. Once these males noticed what a prized object I was to two superstar jocks, they began sniffing around. I kept them dangling easily using MMG, but my seeming popularity only incensed them more.

"Hey, Kelsey, want a ride home?" Burt Liu would call, trying to encircle my waist as we came out of trigonometry last period. I'd smile abstractly, then look down at my watch. "Can't, Burt," I'd shake my head. "I'm waiting for you know who."

"Who?" he'd say.

"Mr. Big," I'd whisper and then giggle, all the while letting my eyes rove through the cars in the parking lot. Burt would grit his teeth and insist I go home with him, but I'd hold firm to the mystery man and let Burt guess who that might be. Then he'd unhappily stalk off to his car, gun the motor, and roar out of the parking lot—leaving me to whistle a little tune and walk quite happily to the bus stop. MMG #21.

Is it any wonder I was gaining more confidence as time went by? A confidence built on tricks and deviousness and plots and counterplots, to be sure, but still enough like the real article to (almost!) make me start believing in myself. Enough other kids were. Including Danny and Steve.

After the mock photo session behind the stadium Friday afternoon, Steve walked me out to the edge of the parking lot. In the hope that the sports editor of the local San Mateo newspaper might get a glimmer of the shots for a story (more quick improvisational thinking on my part), he was wearing an especially nice sweater under a cord jacket. With the late afternoon sun glinting off his hair, he resembled a young centerfold from *Playgirl* magazine. I wasn't dazzled, but half the female population at Balboa was.

"That wasn't so bad now, was it?" I teased him, remembering the tension in his face and body under the constant clicking of my camera. If only he'd known that the frightening camera had been empty of film!

But he only laughed and slid his sports bag into the backseat of his car. "Not bad at all, champ." He smiled at me. "In fact, kind of fun. You know something? You're all right. I think you're so good maybe ole Stevie Wonder himself here may just pop up in the sports pages yet, right?"

"Uh, right," I stammered, feeling guilty at his obvious exuberance. Then I wiped out all the negative feelings—and fast —when I spotted Cal and Taffy walk out of the side exit toward the parking lot. Steve hadn't seen them coming, but I watched Taffy's eyes reduce to slits as she spied me laughing and talking to Steve Nelson, one of *her* crowd. She ignored something Cal was saying in her effort to absorb this little mini-drama more closely. One thing about her expression: It didn't look happy. Although the Girl Wonder didn't realize it yet, this little unknown entity she called Pig Woman was soon going to explode into a bright big beautiful star: the Kelsey Constellation. And before she could blink her phony green eyes, I was going to take another star—Cal Lindsey— right away from her galaxy and put it into orbit in my own.

"Hey, champ," Steve Nelson snapped his fingers in front of my thoughtful face. Little did he know I was light-years away. "Want a ride somewhere? I'm going past Crestwood Boulevard."

Normally, MMG #21 would be enforced at this point, but

seeing Taffy's pinched face and slit eyes locking on to mine, I improvised on the rules. "A ride?" I called in a carrying voice across the parking lot. "Why, thanks, Steve. Love one!" And I hopped in his silver BMW with a small victorious smirk at T. Foster!

✳ nine

If there were one word that could capture my life-style in
the following two weeks, it would assuredly be *fun-omenal!*
There were lunch dates with eager would-be suitors, long
afternoons with the athletic crowd in the prized back booth of
the Deli, and several wild parties at Danny Ortiz's house when
his parents were away. If I was not the LOP (life of the party)
at these affairs, at least I wasn't PNG (persona non grata).
Cal's crowd began accepting me, but primarily out of mistaken
identity. Let me explain. Danny Ortiz asked me to his party
because he thought I was seeing Steve Nelson. Steve Nelson
was all smiles and flirty with me because he thought I was
seeing Danny Ortiz! Taffy Foster was all daggers and dragon
breath to me because she *knew* I was seeing no one!

But the laugh was on her. I moved as easily up the hierarchical ladder of her group as Pharaoh inspecting his latest pyramid. Nothing stopped me now. As MMG #15 had promised (and so beautifully delivered): "Acceptance is merely a trick of appearance." I *appeared* to be someone's friend in her crowd, but just whose, no one could say for sure. It just seemed natural now that I be included in the circle.

I wasn't complaining, mind you. MMG was performing far better than I could have dreamed. Cal Lindsey seemed so much more obtainable now that I knew his friends, and each day at school he seemed to focus on my face a little more clearly. And yet I was feeling decidedly guilty over using the Magic Male Grabbers on John Perry. We had been close friends, and maybe something a little more, but now MMG was pulling us apart. I saw him at the *Galleon* meetings, but it was all business. I was treated like everyone else in the group. No, that's not true. I was treated with a little less warmth, a little less respect. It infuriated me. It made my blood boil. But what could I do? Jeopardize my new power position by letting J.P. know that he got under my skin but good?

No way.

I swallowed my deep feelings like the whale swallowed Jonah. I swallowed the hurt of seeing Beverlee and Sonia brush past me with hurried greetings—and nothing more. I didn't blame them. I had shut all my old friends out. The Ugly Ducklings Anonymous chapter had disbanded, and now there was little to talk about. The friendship was strained even worse one cool Friday afternoon in mid-December.

The last bell had rung and I was quickly heading out the door when someone came up behind me and tapped me on the shoulder. I gave an annoyed start of surprise and then saw that it was Beverlee. Of course she had to apologize over and over again for bothering me, but finally managed to get out what she came to say. She invited me to her house for some junk-food feasting and a talk fest. . . . "Just like old times," she rather wistfully said.

"Oh no, this afternoon?" I mumbled, biting at my lip. I had made arrangements to meet Steve Nelson's current girlfriend, Cindy Ramirez. This was a very important date for me. Little dark-eyed Cindy was one of the Pom-Pom girls, and to create a divisive wedge in that Foster Fortress, I had to try to penetrate defenses. Of course I had promised Cindy a free modeling shoot for her portfolio, so the barter system was in full play. And she had let slip that Cal Lindsey was going to be at the Deli. Without Taffy Foster.

A perfect omen.

Yet here was little kitten Beverlee offering me a chance at reconciliation like a cupcake on a plate. It was a very tempting offer. I had sorely missed my quiet friend's sense of humor and loyal friendship in the past weeks, and I wanted nothing better than to throw up my hands, waggle my expressive eyebrows at her, giggle and say, "Have I got a story for you! It's called Magic Male Grabbers, and it starts with a girl named Priska Rodgers. . . ."

But I didn't. I placed my obsession with Cal Lindsey on one end of a scale and my feelings for Beverlee and Sonia on the other and then stood back and weighed them. As much as I respected and needed friendship, physical lust and romantic excitation in the embodiment of my idol tipped the scales heavily. A chance of revenge against Taffy Foster added still more weight to the deciding vote.

I sighed and apologized to Bev. She heard out my feeble

excuse and then threw in the zinger, "I wouldn't keep harping on it, Kelsey, but it's really for Sonia. It's her birthday today, and this is her surprise party, you see."

I did see. I saw what an uncaring, unfeeling person I was to forget such a dear friend's important day. Just as I was about to tell her exactly what a fool I was and of course, I'd be there, Cal Lindsey came walking toward me with Cindy Ramirez in tow. Instantly all thoughts of Sonia went out of my head. My heart beat crazily against my chest and flew out of my body and danced wildly in front of me. I lost my voice and produced only airless squeaks to Bev. The boy was so fine, so artistically put together, that he seemed to flow in motion like warm honey. The honeypot stopped in front of me and grinned. At me? Dear Lord, right at me!

Then the honeypot opened its gorgeous mouth and said, "Heard you were joining us at the Deli, Kelsey. We've got some other kids lined up who're meeting us there at four. Cindy thought you needed a ride, so do you want to head on over with us before the mob gets there?"

I said, "Oh, yeah, sure. That's great. Yeah, a ride. Right. That's great, yeah . . ."

"What Kelsey's trying to tell us is that she needs a ride, right, Kelsey?" Thank God Cindy interrupted my senseless babbling, otherwise I'd still be there, locked away in a time capsule, nodding my head like an idiot and mumbling, "Uh yeah, great. Fine. A ride? Uh yeah, great. Fine" ad infinitum.

Beverlee made an almost involuntary movement next to me, and I looked over quickly. "But Kelsey," she softly pleaded, "the surprise party!" The sight of her face, the expression in her eyes, wrenched me back to reality in seconds. What was I doing? Was I crazy? Or worse, as shallow and unfeeling as a Taffy Foster? But then an unfortunate vision streaked across my path and made up my mind for me immediately. John Perry was loping along the corridor heading in our direction. As he got closer, I could see his eyes take in the dramatic little grouping, see the lines in his jaw tighten as he noticed me. Instantly, his face closed up, and that alone did it. I was so furious at him that I cooed up to Cal as loudly as I could, "Well, if you want to leave now, what are we waiting around here for?" And I smiled up at the Sexy Senior and leaned close to him.

J.P.'s eyes bulged. His lips thinned. I never before appreciated the acrobatic ability in his features. But then, I had never tried so hard to make him angry. Before I swung off with the Pretty People, I whispered hastily to a stricken Bev that I would try to make the party as soon as I could after I got done at the Deli. That placated her slightly, but it didn't erase the hurt set to her mouth as I gaily caught up with Cal and Cindy and headed out the door.

Look out, Balboa. Watch out, universe. The Kelsey Constellation is shining now!

But fading all too quickly.

The enchanted afternoon with Cal Lindsey never did materialize after all. If someone had told me that Taffy Foster was into black magic and had maliciously, deliberately, thrown a wrench in the works, I would have believed it. Ordinary human events alone couldn't have made the little red Triumph plow merrily and way too forcefully into the back of a VW that was waiting for a light to change. If Cal Lindsey were a god, he certainly didn't have too much power with the police who checked out the accident. We were detained quite a while as Cal and the irate owner of the damaged car exchanged information and the police wrote out a report. Somehow the sizzle slid right off into a fizzle as the afternoon disappeared. By four thirty or so nobody was in the mood for pizza or small talk. An unusually subdued Cal dropped me off at Beverlee's house and then drove away forlornly with Cindy.

So much for constellations, starshine, and magic.

The day got worse when Beverlee opened the door and said coolly, "No one's here anymore. Sonia waited, but when you didn't show up by four thirty, she left."

"Oh, Bev, I'm sorry. I'm really sorry," I said with genuine regret. But not half as sorry as when I got home to find John Perry waiting for me in the living room. My mom had circled the poor boy with plates of cookies, cake, and other junk food, but he wasn't eating a thing. He just sat on the sofa, politely listening to Margaret drone on and on about how well Michael was doing in college. For a brief second in the hallway, when I first heard his voice, my heart contracted. An incredible spasm of happiness danced through my mind and I thought, He's come to apologize to me for being so cold all these weeks. He misses me too much to keep up this ridiculous Cold War. And I entered the living room eagerly.

Then I faltered when I saw the expression in his eyes. They didn't look apologetic or warm at all. Margaret sensed all was not well in Teen Land and for once, quickly excused herself, throwing me an odd look before she disappeared into the kitchen. I forced myself to breathe deeply and to control my nervous hands as J.P. pushed the plates of food away and got to his feet.

"Well, well," I quipped merrily, falsely. "This is an unexpected surprise. A personal visit from John Perry Curtin. To what do I owe the honor?"

"Skip all the cute remarks and social patter," he replied. "You can save all that garbage for your subjects at school.

92

Now the only reason I came over here," he went on, overriding my sputtering anger at his comment, "was to ask you why you failed to show at Sonia's party this afternoon. Was it more important to go off on a social whirl with the 'in' people than to spend an hour or so with people you proclaim your best friends?"

"Oh, come on," I smiled. "This isn't one of Shakespeare's tragedies, you know. So I missed my friend's surprise party. So I'll get her something tomorrow. There won't be any hard feelings, I guarantee."

"Don't count on it. You may be able to laugh off feelings these days and think you can buy friendship with a gift, but I doubt if Sonia or Beverlee can. Sonia was not in the best of moods when I took her home."

I turned away from his probing eyes, shocked by his admission. "*You* took her home. Why?" But I honestly didn't want to hear the answer. I was afraid I already knew.

"Let's just say she was depressed and leave it at that. She cares for you—a lot. Or maybe you didn't realize that. Both girls do. Which surprises the hell out of me, considering the way you've been treating them lately. Don't you care about them at all?"

"Of course I do!" I retorted, and then bit back a more emotional reply. I swallowed and tried not to let a great wave of tears overwhelm me. "I care. But—it's just, well . . ." Words failed me. The tears came anyway, against my will and totally against the dictates of Magic Male Grabbers. Within seconds, my shoulders were quivering, and J.P. moved close behind me.

"Kelsey, what is it?" he murmured, his voice already softening with concern. "Do you think I don't know how much

93

you've changed these past few weeks? I've been watching you. You act so differently now. You're all confidence and smiles and buddy-buddy with the top layer of the pond—"

"What's wrong with that?" I got out in a small voice. Watch out, Marshall, I warned myself. J.P. was dangerously close to me, closer than he'd ever been before, and my body was reacting strangely. I felt tingling and excited and scared, all at the same time.

"There's nothing wrong with any of that," J.P. cried, "if I thought you really liked these people, but friends of Taffy Foster, the girl you love to hate? What happened to Sonia or Beverlee—or even me—to talk to anymore? What happened to the Kelsey who was confused and insecure, but still a special friend?"

He gently turned me around. I hurriedly wiped my eyes, but I know I must have been a soggy wreck.

"She's still here," I said softly, relaxing under his warm gaze. "You just stopped looking for her."

"I didn't stop, wet eyes." J.P. shook his head and took my hand. "You never let me get close. To talk to Kelsey Marshall now means you have to make an appointment weeks in advance and first put your request in writing."

"Oh, it does not!" I giggled, perfectly content to stand there and smile at J.P.'s wonderful face, those lean features and soft spaniel-eyes that melted my icy heart. It felt so good to be holding his hand and gently squeezing it, his strong fingers intertwining with mine. I was losing control. I was melting into a pool of foolish water right at the boy's feet. What had happened to my Magic Male Grabbers? Suddenly, there didn't seem to be a need to pit my will against J.P.'s. We were in total harmony, two close individuals who liked each other *equally*. It was a shock to me, but a happy one. It felt liberating. No lying or devious tricks or traps. No sneaky maneuvering to keep him on his toes.

What happened next was even more wonderful. J.P. helped wipe away the last of my tears and then let one finger slowly trace its way down my cheek—where it stopped, hesitantly, by my lips. I was trembling so hard now out of wonder and excitement that I didn't stop him when he gently outlined my lips with his fingers.

"You've got the most adorable mouth," he sighed. "When it's not coming out with anything caustic or silly, that is!" And he leaned down and oh-so-slowly, oh-so-surely kissed me. It was a warm, light, tender kiss—yet it rocked me anyway. There was something so special in it that my heart began pounding in my chest. J.P. looked down at me seriously.

"You feel it, too?" he asked.

I could only nod my head, too shaken to respond.

"Good," he said. "We'll have to explore that. When I don't have a swim-meet practice scheduled in"—he hurriedly checked his watch—"oh, thirty minutes from now! Maybe after school one of these days?"

I nodded once more, too scared and puzzled and happy over what had just transpired to trust myself to say anything. With a tender smile and a wave of my hand, I watched J.P. go in a rainbow of feelings. I whirled around the room and hurled soft pillows in delight. I couldn't believe that a *friendship* could grow into something this exciting, this different. And it hadn't needed Magic Male Grabbers to make the magical transformation! With that thought in mind, I began humming softly and went into the kitchen to help Mags start dinner.

✳ ten

I didn't see John Perry Curtin again for a week.

The very next day one of his teachers called him and asked him to substitute for a sick friend at a Junior United Nations Conference in New York. Within an hour he had packed a bag and was at the airport. The conference took a whole lonely week. Those seven days without him gave me a chance to replay our last little scene together over and over, visualizing the original fiery anger in his eyes change to the softly hypnotic warmth and vulnerability I like so much.

Of course I had to do instant replays of our first kiss. Every time I thought about the way his lips felt on mine, I got all shivery. I kept daydreaming in biology and French and during lunch about the way J.P.'s arms would feel around me, the way his hand would feel holding mine.

I was too delirious. I can't say I stopped using Magic Male Grabbers completely the week J.P. was in New York, but somehow I was so naturally high all the time and so radiant that I didn't seem to need to lie. I didn't forget Cal Lindsey, either. That's like saying I forgot about the sun or breathing. The kind of mammoth crush that I had on him just doesn't disappear in a matter of days. Yet I found myself questioning the depth of my feeling toward my blond cowboy with the macho squint when I was now daydreaming about John Perry Curtin.

The Friday that J.P. flew home, I came home from school chattering merrily to Sonia. I had listened to John Perry and made the effort to win my two friends back. But how Sonia could remain friends with someone who talked nonstop about J.P. was beyond me! I left her, then raced home to ask my mom if J.P. had phoned to tell me he'd landed. Mags was on the phone all right, but not with John Perry. She was talking to Michael, and I could tell that something was terribly wrong. I hung up my coat and sidled close to her, silently mouthing "What's wrong?" at periodic frustrating intervals. Without an explanation, her expression changed, and she thrust the phone at me. "Here," she snapped, "it's *your* friend."

"Hello?" I said. "Mike? Is something wrong?"

And then heard a sly little tinkle of laughter. "Nothing's wrong at all, Kelsey," said Priska. "In fact, everything's just perfect. Your brother and I are going strong. But I want to hear about you. What's been happening with MMG?"

To Margaret's bafflement, I briefly outlined the various tricks I had used. Then, in a burst of general joyousness, I confided in her about J.P. "No more games now, Priska," I exclaimed. "We like each other in just the same way."

"This is *exactly* the right time to use all the later MMGs, the ones toward the end. The ones I call the jealousy cluster. You can't start fast enough. Seriously, Kelsey. How long do you think this euphoric state between you will last if you don't help it along? Do some thinking. Fast." She went on some more about the necessity of using her methods, and as I was wavering, Michael came on the line.

"You can't believe how nutty I am about this woman, Kelsey." He laughed. I could hear Priska giggling in the background. "I don't know what she's been telling you, but if it's about guys and how to please them, then you better listen to her. The woman knows what she's talking about!" He babbled on about his adored Priska for several more minutes until I finally got him off the phone. When I did, Margaret came bustling in and stood in front of me, distress puckering her face.

"Did you hear that, Kelsey?" she moaned. "Michael's thinking of getting married to that—that *creature.* He's thinking about ruining his life by getting tied down at his age. Why, my baby is just eighteen!" I commiserated briefly with Mags, but had something far more important to do. I raced upstairs and pulled out the little black notebook. I turned to the jealousy cluster tricks Priska had mentioned and thoroughly read them through. I would need them, it seemed, to ignite J.P.'s spark and keep our relationship exciting.

But everything was going so well without them, a small inner voice complained. Why do you need them now?

Because I want things to be even *better*! I angrily whispered back and then shut out the voice to concentrate on memorizing the tricks. When J.P. called later that afternoon, I instructed a baffled Margaret to tell him I had come home from school, but had gone out again with Steve Nelson. That piece of news should drive him crazy, I thought. Now he'll be dying to see me!

Apparently the little trick worked perfectly because J.P. called me later that night and told me how much he wanted to see me. Would Saturday morning be all right? I took a moment to answer, as if pawing through a huge social calendar, and then giggled. "Saturday morning's out—I made other plans—but the afternoon is free."

J.P. said fine, he'd be over at one, and then he hung up rather abruptly.

Saturday morning I took the notebook downstairs with me and studied it over breakfast. Then I borrowed money from Mags and called the local florist to have a bouquet of flowers sent. Oh, not to J.P. to welcome him back, but to me!

MAGIC MALE GRABBER #26: Whenever the romance is waning, secretly send yourself flowers with an unsigned card. Then conveniently arrange to have your boyfriend present so he can see the flowers arrive—and your delighted expression. He'll be green with jealousy.

J.P. wasn't green at all, but the color of his face did change when the florist's delivery boy followed him up the steps to my house at one and announced he had a bouquet for me.

"Oh, J.P.," I sighed eagerly, ripping off the paper around the flowers. "You shouldn't have! These are lovely. Really lovely."

J.P. stared at me and the emerging baby roses blankly. But as he began to scowl and stammer out protestations, I hurriedly left the room to get a vase. Leaving him alone, of course, with my opened card lying out on the table. The card said, "Thinking of you." When I returned, triumphantly bearing the roses in a vase, he was looking at me with a strange, unsmiling expression on his face. "Well, Kelsey," he began softly, "did you have a nice week when I was away?"

"Nice?" I gaily repeated, raising my coy eyebrows at him. "Let's say it was more *busy* than anything else."

"Doing what?" His voice was still soft, his eyes still holding mine.

Why, I thought, he's furiously jealous of the person who sent me the roses. He's trying to find out just who the unknown admirer really is! This was better than I expected. A feeling of power flooded through me as I realized how much John Perry cared for me. "Well," I smiled almost shyly, "you know how crazy December can be at our school. Everyone's thinking of Christmas vacation and throwing parties and doing insane things after school."

"And of course, since you've become so popular and such a little whirlwind, everyone asked you to all these—insane—things . . . ?"

His tone was light, casual, but a vague uneasiness settled over me. Then I inwardly admonished myself for being so dramatic, and nodded, taking the vase and placing it on the mantel. Up there it commanded far greater attention. It seemed to symbolize the whole passionate meaning of Magic Male Grabbers. I adjusted the baby's breath slightly and then turned back to face J.P., who seemed to radiate tension as I walked over to him. It appeared for one second that he drew back from me as I reached out to take his hand, but then I knew I must be wrong when he suggested we take in a movie at the old Rialto theater downtown. I quickly and happily agreed. Hadn't MMG #26 worked out perfectly?

And once John Perry Curtin was truly all mine, then maybe MMG would help me get Cal Lindsey—and others, too. Oh, I know. You can't have your cake and eat it too. Right? Wrong! I've always been blessed with a large appetite. I was sure I could accommodate many desserts.

For now, however, I wanted to concentrate on John Perry. He and I liked each other a lot; in fact, the more time we spent together, the more we cared for each other. But the odd part is that we actually spent very little time together! During the next couple of weeks, when J.P. would set a date for us to meet, I'd break it to ensure his interest and keep him wondering who I was seeing instead. MMG #18. The funny part about all this was his reaction. Somehow, Magic Male Grabbers didn't seem to work on him the way they did on my brother, Michael, or on any of the other guys at school who had buzzed around me. I'd cancel a date with J.P. or be too busy to see him and instead of being hurt or jealous, he'd simply hear me out and then grin. "Guess it's all for the best," he'd say, lightly tapping my nose. "I'm pretty involved myself. I could use the time doing other things."

I wanted so desperately to believe he was busy with his family over the Christmas break, but I had to wonder. My holidays were spent overindulging, returning gifts, and imagining what J.P. was up to. Not that I'd call him—MMG #8.

I growled and scowled in private, but didn't realize something was up until the *Galleon* meeting the first Wednesday afternoon back at school. It was January 5, only a week and a half away from the big Sno-Ball, Balboa's most popular dance of the year. A king was elected at the event and he, in turn, got to choose his queen from a bevy of five princesses. The whole student body had been talking about the upcoming event for weeks, and I had just assumed J.P. would be going with me. True, he hadn't asked me yet and true, whenever I'd bring up the dance he'd smile in sphinxlike manner and change the subject. When I stopped to think about it, the guy was slowly driving me crazy. I wasn't all that sure anymore where I stood with him. If Magic Male Grabbers were supposed to bring us closer, then why, oh why, were they pulling us apart? J.P. just didn't respond in the usual manner. I discovered the reason the afternoon of the yearbook meeting.

It was a day I want to erase from the blackboard of my life. I walked into the staff office to discover J.P. laughing and talking with Taffy Foster! He was sitting at the head of the old table where he always sits, but the spot usually reserved for me was taken by the Blonde Blob. I choked back an expression of outrage and walked quickly to where the two were talking. Jim Orr, my faithful admirer at the meetings, jumped up when he saw me and pointed to the empty chair near him. I shot J.P. a meaningful, hurt look, but he only glanced up, gave me a brief, distracted "Hi" and went right on babbling. I was furious. I slid in next to Jim and tried to mask my anger, but it was hard going. Especially when he called over to J.P., "Hey, almighty leader! Are you recruiting Pom-Pom girls for the yearbook now?"

Taffy flashed him a golden-glow smile that singed my eyebrows, and I was horrified to hear J.P. say, "You got it, Jim. In fact—hey! c'mon, everybody, settle down!—I want to introduce you to the *Galleon*'s newest member—"

"And prettiest!" some drooling male inserted.

"—Taffy Foster."

102

"And just what is Taffy Foster going to be doing for us?" I asked, too enraged to keep still. "Writing a feature column on football stars? Or maybe doing a special retrospective on the Pom-Pom uniform—how it's changed in the past fifteen years?"

There was a catty note to my voice, but I didn't care. J.P. couldn't be serious. He just couldn't. What he said next, however, proved to me just how dead serious he was. "As a matter of fact," he said coolly, very distinctly, "Taffy wants to help with the photographic end of things. And as everyone knows only too well, we're shorthanded in this area. Kelsey, I'm assigning you to work with Taffy, teach her how to use the Nikon. There's a basketball game between Balboa and Burlingame coming up this Friday night. This is the perfect opportunity for the two of you to work together. I'll be looking forward to seeing how Taffy's pictures turn out."

NO NO NO NO NO! J.P. couldn't be doing this to me. He just *couldn't.* He knew how I felt about Taffy. He knew exactly how I felt. But The $64,000 Question was: How did he feel about *her?*

I didn't know. I never saw them together before, but that didn't mean he couldn't be friends with her when I wasn't around. And lately, Sonia and Beverlee hadn't seen much of J.P., so I couldn't pump them. Lord knows, with my Magic Male Grabber treatment, I gave Taffy and J.P. both plenty of opportunity to flirt, laugh, or make fools of themselves with each other without me ever knowing.

Somehow I got through the meeting without bursting into tears or leaping for Taffy's slender throat. I kept furtively stealing peeks at her, but she never once looked my way. Her little cat eyes were fixed on John Perry's face. In fact, she seemed fixated on his whole body. I didn't like the vibrations I was getting from that end of the table. It would be just like her to go after J.P. now that she knew we were dating. But J.P. was no wax dummy, no store mannequin to be so easily manipulated. He had a mind and a mouth to say no to her. If he wanted to, that is. That was the problem! Did he want to?

As soon as the meeting broke up, I lingered, talking to some friends, but keeping my eyes on the duo at the front. Would they *never* stop laughing? Never stop flirting? Ugh. When Jim Orr eagerly asked me out for a pizza, I started to refuse when something stopped me. W-a-i-t a minute. Maybe this was what J.P. needed: a shot in the arm that said "Better take care of your girl before someone else does." So I hooked Jim's arm in mine and advanced on J.P. and Taffy.

"Sorry to break into your cozy tête-à-tête," I interrupted, "but I wanted to ask Taffy to meet me at the North Gate on Friday night by six thirty. That way we should have plenty of time to work on the camera before the game starts."

Taffy barely glanced at me, she was so entranced in whatever J.P. had been telling her. "Fine," she nodded, giving her long blonde hair an impatient shake.

"Oh, and J.P.? I just wanted to let you know that Jim wants me to go for pizza with him." The statement was more of a question than anything else, if he was really listening to what I was saying.

"Is that what you really want to do?" John Perry asked me, throwing the ball neatly in my court and finally meeting my eyes. The warmth and desire that I once saw there were clouded under a blanket of snow. He was so abominably cool, so abominably uncaring, that I squeezed Jim's arm and defiantly smiled.

"That's exactly what I intend to do," I said.

104

J.P. glanced quickly at Taffy, who artfully, innocently, beamed up at him. "All this talk about pizza is making me hungry. What do you say, Taffy? How about a nice Chinese dinner tonight, say at Hunan's?" I clenched and unclenched my fists as Taffy agreed, and I walked out of the room with J.P. calling after me, "Oh, Kelsey, have fun!"

He infuriated me. He drove me mad. If this was a relationship, it was an awfully painful one. All I wanted to do was make him like me *more,* and now it seemed I was losing him to the worst person possible: Balboa High's answer to Vampira. Was it the tricks that had failed me—or simply J.P.? Maybe he never really did care for me the way I cared for him. Otherwise he'd be terribly jealous right now and beating out Jim Orr for a dinner date.

I was all confused. Something had gone disastrously wrong. The thought of eating pizza and practicing more MMG bored and sickened me. I just couldn't do it. I made up an excuse to Jim and stood in the darkening corridor, watching him fade away in the twilight and feeling like the loneliest, unhappiest person on earth. Ten minutes later, J.P. and Taffy came strolling out of the staff office, and I hurriedly moved down the hall so they wouldn't see me. Taffy had her hand lightly on J.P.'s arm and they were talking animatedly about the Sno-Ball as they pushed out into the parking lot.

I was still standing there fifteen minutes later, the tears blurring my eyes, when Cal Lindsey found me.

❊ eleven

It's so funny. You can dream about something and fantasize about it and have it planned perfectly in your head. But when Reality strikes with a capital *R*, out flies the movie script. For nearly fifteen months I had made Cal Lindsey the guiding light in my life. If that sounds a bit like a soap opera, that's exactly how I felt. I kept clippings of him in my diary, I daydreamed about him endlessly, and I invented thousands of scenarios where he would find me alone somewhere, distressed, in tears, and he'd take a good hard look at my sweet face and murmur—

"EXCUSE ME! Has Taffy Foster come out of the *Galleon* meeting yet?"

So much for the daydream! Here was hard, brutal reality.

But somehow, after the depressing scene I had just been through with J.P., I couldn't get myself all worked up and dewy-eyed over this blond vision. I was too drained. I wiped my eyes and almost managed to sound as if I had a bad cold when I said, "Taffy's gone. She left nearly twenty minutes ago."

"Left?" Cal took a step closer to me. "What do you mean? That's impossible. What are you doing out here? Isn't the meeting still going on?"

"Finished nearly twenty minutes ago," I said, watching his beautiful face take in the implications of what I had told him.

"But—but Taffy. What happened to Taffy? She and I have a date scheduled for right after this meeting. . . ."

"Not anymore you don't." I straightened up and blew my nose.

"You mean . . ." He stopped, but from the way his eyes were clicking I could tell he knew what was going on. And who with.

"That's right," I finished bitterly. "She went off. With J.P. Your friend and my friend—reaching a new level of friendship together, it seems."

I meant to be flippant and uncaring, but it really wasn't funny at all. It hurt terribly. And I was amazed to see that Cal felt the exact same way. I guess there's no accounting for tastes, but my macho cowboy had fallen for the plastic princess —hard. Well, that made two of us. I had fallen for J.P.

As I said, your own private movie script gets tossed pretty quickly when you're confronted by the real thing. What could two unhappy people like us do except get together and commiserate? I certainly didn't intend to stand around the deserted hallway all evening, a soggy Kleenex in my hand, moaning endlessly about John Perry. First of all, the maintenance crew would have kicked me out. And second—I was starved!

So, apparently, was Mr. Lindsey. It's amazing how hunger and a romantically depressed state can bring two people together. We both discussed the inexpensive restaurants in the area, until he raked a hand through his hair and cried, "The hell with eating cheap tonight! This calls for a huge meal at a great place. Er, my treat, of course."

We ended up at Ernie's in San Francisco.

That had to be one of the most elegant, most beautiful, most *expensive* restaurants around! While Cal called ahead for reservations, I called my mom. Margaret started in on the guilt machine midway through my explanation (". . . and you're never around this house anymore. And how do you think I feel, all alone, waiting for you to come home? I was going to make a special dinner tonight, the one you like so much, but now . . ." whine—whine—whine), but I refused to play the game and quickly hung up. Maybe in a very perverse way, Magic Male Grabbers were teaching me to behave in a less babyish, more assertive way. Lord knows, I was calmly going off with the school's most sexy creature to have an intimate dinner at Ernie's. And I wasn't experiencing heart palpitations —yet!

I never did.

Who would have imagined that a softly romantic, candlelit dinner à deux would irrevocably burst my bubble about Cal Lindsey! But all through the hushed, reverential meal where waiters glided in and out like nuns, and the incomparable culinary delights melted on my palate like hot fudge topping, I kept thinking about one thing and one thing only: John Perry

Curtin! Cal would ask me something about myself, and instead of being flattered by his attention and all giggly and goggle-eyed, I'd answer matter-of-factly. Inside, I was wondering if J.P. were still in Taffy's company and if so, what he was doing! Was he sitting in a booth somewhere with her, his face close to hers? Was he laughing at something she was saying, his eyes on hers with that concentrated, warm look—

Oh! I couldn't stand it! I threw down my napkin and felt hot tears prickling the back of my eyes. Instantly, Cal put down his fork and reached across the table to take my hand. "Don't think about it, Kelsey. Remember? We promised to have a wonderful time and not think about—them."

"I can't help it," I cried, pulling my hand from Cal's grip. It wasn't J.P.'s hand. It didn't feel the same way. "That's *all* I'm able to think about. Aren't you?"

He didn't have to answer. The wounded puppy-dog look in his blue eyes told all. Puppy-dog look . . . puppies. The very thought of canine creatures instantly brought to mind Magic Male Grabbers and Priska's cool view of men as dogs on a leash. Perhaps by putting our muzzles together, Cal and I could come up with a doggoned good idea.

"Listen," I commanded Cal, leaning across the table in my enthusiasm. "How much do you like Cotton—er, Taffy? I mean, how much do you want her back?"

"Why?" His hangdog features brightened. "Do you have an idea?"

"I just might," I said, with a small smile.

Could this really be Kelsey Marshall, formerly of Pig Woman fame, exchanging ideas and sorrow with Cal Lindsey as if he were a close *friend* and not the unattainable god she had always painted him? Incredible. And yet true. Over a delicious dessert of chocolate mousse and coffee, we explored the idea of forming a temporary alliance in order to make our respective loves jealous. When I mentioned the Sno-Ball, Cal hesitated. I didn't mean to be cruel, but I had to spell it out to him. "Listen, just this afternoon, I overheard Taffy and J.P. discussing the Sno-Ball. Now, I don't know if you two have a firm commitment to go together, but J.P. has certainly not asked me. So I'm free. Now what about you?"

Cal thrust out his adorable lower lip in a sulky pout. "Well, actually, she never told me she'd definitely go with me. She's been kind of putting it off. So, well, oh hell! I'm free!"

"Then I suggest we make it known around school that we'll be going together. And if that doesn't bring J.P. and Taffy to their senses, I don't know what will."

Cal threw me a tentative grin. "OK. You're the boss. It sounds like you know exactly what you're doing. But Kelsey, I have to ask"—the candlelight on the table shadowed his face, creating stormy tide pools in his normally sunny blue eyes—"what if this plan doesn't work out? I mean, what if it backfires in our faces and we push them even closer together?"

"Then they're really fools who deserve each other!"

We both laughed, but deep inside I knew too well my batting average with MMG. I privately agonized over this little scheme. Oh, J.P., I prayed, I have to believe that you really do care for me. That the kiss we shared was really a promise of something special to come.

When Cal dropped me off, I was, if not a happier girl, then certainly a chubbier one. "Remember our plan!" I whispered to him just before he roared off. His answering smile was a ghostly glow in the lights from the dashboard, but he gave me a thumbs-up sign. "Please let this work," I muttered as I turned to my house.

But I got such a disheartening omen when I went in that it should have warned me off this devious plan as well as all other MMGs, now and forevermore. I knew the minute I stepped inside that something was wrong. For one thing, I could hear my father blustering away at somebody in the den. But it wasn't Mags he was yelling at because she was opening the door. "Oh, Kelsey," she mumbled, quickly drawing me in. "It's awful. Just awful. Your father is so angry he could explode."

"What's awful?" I asked, tossing my jacket and books on the sofa, then facing my mom. "Tell me!"

"It's Michael. My baby. He wants to quit school. Your father's really having a fit about it. Can you hear him?"

Not only could *I* hear him, but I'm sure all the neighbors on Kenwood Avenue could as well. "But why? I thought Mike liked school. He was doing so well. . . ."

"That's just the point. He wasn't doing that well. He just hid it from us. He got in with that—that vixen creature, and she took up all his free time, made him her little slave—you saw it, remember?—and his grades suffered. Now she's threatening to drop him for someone else, and he's going crazy. He wants to leave school."

"WHAT!" I couldn't believe my ears. The perfect relationship shattered to pieces? Priska having the nerve to dump my brother, who loved her and treated her royally, for someone else? It sounded suspiciously too much like Magic-Male-Grabber time. Well, this time she picked the wrong person to manipulate. It just so happened that I knew her little game because she had taught me so well. And I just knew I could

111

beat her at it. But I had to knock some sense into Michael's head first.

"Ma," I whispered. "Don't worry. Michael will stay in school. I think I know how to keep him there. Just do me a favor and send him on up to me when he's done being chewed out by Dad. If there's anything left on his bones, that is!"

I raced up the stairs, determined to make Michael see that his adorable little love object was really a cold and calculating witch. In order to do that, I wanted to show him the tangible evidence: the more than fifty Magic Male Grabbers Priska had given me, which were now bound up in a little black notebook. I flew through the door to my bedroom, headed straight for the drawer where I usually kept the notebook and reached in under my underwear to discover—nothing! The book was gone.

I couldn't understand it. Whatever could have happened to it? I went through my room like a whirling dervish, turning drawers and closets inside out, but still, nothing. I went through all my pockets, because for a while there I had taken the notebook with me to school. Again, zero. Oh, my God. School. I must have dropped it in school somewhere, in gym or one of my classes. I bit my lip and sat down weakly, my heart already racing in horror. Maybe by now someone had found it and had turned it in to our Lost and Found. But I doubted it. One peek inside the little cover was dynamite. No one would readily give up that kind of information. Oh, Lord. Whatever could I do?

I was on my hands and knees combing the littered floor around the bed when Michael's disconsolate face peeked in. "Hi, Kel," he mumbled in a little-boy, caved-in voice. "Mom said you wanted to see me."

It broke my heart. I knew only too well now what he was

going through. So I brushed off my hands and knees, got up, and invited him in.

"Michael," I said, settling on my bed and pointing him to a chair, "I think we have a lot to talk about. Have you ever heard about Magic Male Grabbers. . . ?"

✻ twelve

Thursday turned out to be the kind of day most suitable for staying at home in bed, watching all the soap operas, and committing junk-food hara-kiri. Unfortunately, I had to tempt my fate and go off to Balboa in the morning like a French aristocrat meeting her fate at the guillotine. I was still heartsick and jealous over J.P.'s sudden hunger for brainless Cotton Candy. And more than that, I was worried sick that someone at school had found my MMG book and was now awaiting the chance to publicly ridicule me with it.

It was with a sinking feeling in my stomach that I walked away from the Lost and Found office. Kindly Mrs. Fernando assured me that a little black notebook was nowhere to be found on her shelves. Some assurance! The old saying "No news is good news" certainly did not apply in this case. I wanted *desperately* to have my hands on that explosive information. It didn't take much soul searching to realize how ashamed I was about playing the control game with Magic Male Grabbers. First it almost cost me my friendship with Sonia and Beverlee. Now it was threatening to play havoc with my relationship with J.P. I wasn't very proud of myself on that dismal Thursday morning. I wanted more than anything else to find John Perry and throw myself at his mercy, to confess all to him—the lies, the tricks and game playing— and then beg his forgiveness. But even more important, I wanted to look him in the eyes and tell him that I was crazy about him and only him, that I liked and respected him as a friend as well as a boyfriend, and that I wanted us to grow into the special couple we were on the brink of becoming that one magical day he kissed me.

But I was scared.

Either J.P. was avoiding me all day Thursday and Friday or he was extremely busy. "Why don't you call him?" Beverlee urged me. "This is the era of women's emancipation. We're not still in the feudal days." But I couldn't. I started to dial his number several times on Thursday night, but I was too frightened to complete the call. What if he were out with Taffy? Or Amy Lanier? What if he came to the phone with a note of rejection in his voice when he knew who it was?

No, I couldn't risk it. It would be too painful. Yet what could be more painful than how I felt *right now*? And who knows? Maybe J.P. felt just as bad as I did and wasn't seeking me out because he was scared, too. With a lightening of spirits, I vowed I would confront him at the *Galleon* staff party Saturday night at the Deli. The Balboa yearbook staff always celebrated a new year in this way, and I was looking forward to a little festivity. Naturally, Cal was going with me (as incentive to Taffykins), but now I only wanted J.P. as my date. It is an ironic world, isn't it!

I spent most of Saturday conferring with my two clothes consultants, Sonia and Beverlee. Dresses were looked at and hurled on the bed, tops and blouses were pawed through and discarded until we had coordinated the most gorgeous outfit: a sexy little cream bouclé sweater shot through with strands of gold, worn loosely over dressy crepe-de-chine black pants. Sonia loaned me a delicate gold necklace. And with lacy black sandals and a small clutch bag, I thought I looked, if not *Vogue* material, then *Glamour* assuredly!

I walked downstairs and paraded for my father, who hugged me suddenly and fiercely. I knew I looked good when Mags started crying. That was the real test. My mother's sobs accompanied me to the door when Cal came to get me. "Oh, my baby! What happened to my own little baby?"

My father grimaced at me. "Better get going, kid. And have a good time, the both of you."

I wish I could say we did.

It all began on such a good note. Cal looked sensational in a sand-colored linen blazer and light blue shirt that emphasized the brilliance of his eyes and highlighted his streaked blond hair. For just a second, as we got out of the car, I felt a glimmer of my infatuation threaten to engulf me again. But it was just a glimmer, and it quickly faded when I realized that my idol had clay feet. Or rather, a blank area in his brain. He adored the school's most gorgeous nitwit, didn't he? No, he was not the man for me. But then, as he grinned a nervous "All set?" look in my direction, I realized that J.P. might have the very same blank area in his brain. Oh no, I breathed, as Cal opened the door to the Deli and we entered the noisy room, please let that not be true!

116

We made a beautiful entrance—as befitting a beautiful couple. So everyone told us, over and over. There was a trace of shock and envy on the girls' faces, but Taffy's, unfortunately, revealed nothing. Of course, that wasn't anything new where she was concerned, but I think Cal would have enjoyed seeing some distress or unhappiness mirrored in his beloved's eyes. She had something else in her vision that evening: John Perry Curtin.

As editor of the yearbook, he was busy playing host and circulating among the small mob that jammed the back room. Even in the dim glow from the Christmas-tree lights that were still in place over the "feast" table, I could see how great he looked. He was not your *Gentlemen's Quarterly* type or the Coors-beer macho male, but an elusive and tantalizing blend of Peter Pan, Warren Beatty, and the powerful Egyptian boy-king Tut!

He had the build of a swimmer and the strength of a wrestler. I had never really ogled him properly until now—when the outcome of the evening was hanging by a thread. Cal was muscular, tall and big-shouldered, a blond appetizer to nibble on before the main course—J.P.!

Compact and energetic, lean and mean, John Perry was the dark heart of the filet mignon, all brown hair and eyes and lightly tanned skin. The expression in his eyes, intense and concentrated, made my heart start doing push-ups and then go off into deep knee bends when he smiled.

He was doing a lot of that now, I saw, watching him filling glasses and joking with his friends. Would he hold on to the smile when he caught up to me? Or would it fade into a cool stare and a "How are you?" and nothing more?

He did neither.

He caught me completely off guard by bringing me a glass

of punch, with a thoughtful expression in his eyes that was neither cold and rejecting nor warm and welcoming. A blend, somewhere in between. Cal, meanwhile, was off, mooning around Taffy but looking far from confident or happy. At least J.P. hadn't spent much time in the Pom-Pom Queen's court that evening. And that realization, combined with the overture in a glass of punch, suddenly lifted my sagging spirits.

"Hi," J.P. said with a solemn wink. "Having a good time?"

I shrugged, trying so desperately to play it cool yet let J.P. know how much I missed him. He quirked an eyebrow.

"I'm not good at translating body language, Kelsey! Would you put that in English?"

"Oh," I took a sip of the cool, fruity liquid and hesitated, "it means that the person I really want to be with hasn't been paying me much attention."

The little muscle I liked so much in his jaw tightened, and he frowned slightly. "And why do *you* think he hasn't?"

My stomach started tightening up, and I felt a number of butterflies smash blindly against my inner walls. Careful, kiddo, I warned myself. Easy does it. We were still skirting the issue, but at least we were starting to talk. I took a deep breath, said a silent prayer, and then let go.

"Because he doesn't know how much I like him, how I think he's special."

J.P. edged closer to me. He said in a restrained voice, "Oh, I don't know. I think he does. And I think he's crazy about you, too." There was something going on beneath the light words J.P. and I were batting back and forth. His eyes were soft and thoughtful—and sad. If I didn't know this boy so well, I would swear he was struggling to maintain his composure. But it didn't make any sense. Why ever should he fight for that if we had just confessed to each other how much we cared about each other? Since we were being so open, I decided to take confession time one step further and tell J.P. about MMG.

"J.P., I'd like to say something to you, but I'm afraid you're going to be—"

I was groping for the right word when he interjected "Hurt?"

"No. More like angry, or furious. It has to do with Cal Lindsey. Oh, I don't know where to start. . . ."

J.P.'s brooding eyes scanned the room and found the blond superstar. It was easy to locate him in that jostling mass of laughing and dancing kids because he was talking angrily to Taffy and waving his arms about. Oh no, I groaned. The plan wasn't working at all for him. She was infuriating him with her indifference—not chasing him with jealousy. And he was making matters worse by losing his cool. MMG #34. Oops.

J.P. shook his head and put a finger to my lips. "No, I don't need to know anything about Cal, Kelsey, or about the both of you. I think I already know. You've just told me now, and something else proved it to me better than words ever could. I just couldn't accept it before."

Startled and confused, I could only stare at J.P., who fumbled in his pocket and produced a small, inexpertly wrapped gift. "Here," he muttered, thrusting it roughly at me. "This is for you. Go on, open it. I was so angry before that I meant to have you open it in front of everyone here tonight, but now I think it's better if you do it in private. I guess I just can't stay mad at you, as much as I'd like to."

Now I was completely baffled. And more than that, scared. Whatever he had wrapped for me was *not* a gift given out of love and affection. It was meant to hurt me. I nervously ripped the paper off, but hesitated when the gleam of black leather winked up at me. The lost MMG notebook! My Magic Male Grabbers! With reddening cheeks, I took it out of the wrapping and held it tightly in my hand. J.P. stood quietly in front of me, his hands clenched into fists by his side. There was a stormy look in his brown eyes. When he spoke, his voice was ragged. "That little book of yours proved to me, more than anything, who you really liked. I didn't believe it at first. Oh, I didn't want to believe it because I liked you so much and I felt that you were starting to care for me—"

"I do! Oh, J.P., I do!" I interrupted, but he cut off my words.

"But these tricks, Kelsey, were all a game plan to trap one person. And that person was Cal Lindsey, not me. I picked up the book out of curiosity, it looked just like the *Galleon*'s financial notebook—that was the day after I came back from New York and you received those damned flowers, right in front of me, and while you were out of the room fixing them, I opened to the first page to check, and there were all these unbelievable tricks and lies. And I saw one about sending yourself flowers! I realized as soon as I saw that that's what you had done to me. I slid the book in my pocket so I could study it later, maybe get a handle on you. Oh, I'm not proud of myself, but believe me, I was going crazy. Here I had just returned from being away a week and anxious to see you, when I learn that you had gone out with Steve Nelson and God knows who else while I was away. And then I read this little book and learned all your tricks, and I saw red. Because you were playing games with all the kids at school to get to one person, and that person is Cal Lindsey. I remembered how you used to rant and rave about Cal when you were still talking to me, but I never thought you'd carry it this far—to use *me* to make him jealous!"

"Stop it! Stop it, J.P.!" I cried, feeling sick inside. "You're all wrong. You've got it all mixed up."

"Do I?" he asked bitterly. "Do I really, *friend*? Isn't that what you kept rubbing in all along? How much you liked me as a friend? Only I didn't buy it. I didn't want to. I felt there was so much more going on between us. But it was always Cal you wanted all along. Not me. I was just convenient to make him jealous. Well, no more. You've won. Taffy tells me that Cal invited you to be his date for the Sno-Ball. Isn't that what you've dreamed of? I wish you two well. From the looks of things, Cal will probably be elected king and then you'll be his queen for the night. Quite a fantasy come true for a girl who used to think she was fat and ugly. But you're not, Kelsey. You never were. I'm just sorry you felt you had to use these stupid games to get what you wanted."

Out of the corner of my eye I could see a furious Cal making his way over to me. I shoved the little black book in my purse and whispered to J.P., "Can't we talk? Somewhere alone? There's so much you don't understand about all this, J.P., and I want you to know how I feel. . . ."

J.P. thrust his hands in his pockets and calmly, distantly, smiled at me. "Oh, you've made it perfectly clear to me and everyone else at school how you feel. I don't think you and I have too much more to say, do we? Since I refuse to be used in your games anymore, you'll have to get yourself a substitute to keep Cal jealous and on his toes. Which one was that, Kelsey? MMG #27? Or was it #28? Oh well, here comes your date now. Have a nice evening. And I'm glad we finally had the chance to talk honestly to each other."

I felt the miles stretch out between us as J.P. walked away.

For the rest of that dismal evening, J.P. stuck close to a few friends, one of whom was Taffy Foster. Cal and I kept up the pretense of being the New Young Lovers, but it was hard going. Both of us slow danced with each other with dreams of two other people in our arms. And both of us talked of only J.P. and Taffy and what they were doing to us. When the party finally broke up around midnight, Taffy playfully grabbed J.P. and led him to some mistletoe left over from Christmas, that was hanging above the door. I watched as she gave him a long and lingering kiss. And he, after struggling jokingly, seemed to relax and enjoy it! Oh, it was hateful! The last straw.

In embarrassed silence, Cal drove me home but turned to me after he pulled up at the curb. "Listen, Kelsey, tonight was the worst, I know, for both of us, but . . ." His voice trailed off as he tapped on the steering wheel.

"But?" I wearily prompted.

"But you are still going to the Sno-Ball with me, aren't you? I mean, I think I can still make Taffy jealous if you go as my date. I think she's hoping that I'll break down and beg her to go with me at the last minute, and I'm not going to. Besides, you and J.P.—"

"Are finished! Kaput. Kelsey and J.P. are no more," I angrily interrupted, then softened as I saw the look in Cal's blue eyes. "Hey, never fear. I'm loyal to my friends. Of course, I'll still go to the Sno-Ball with you, and I hope it all works out the way you want, but J.P. has made it perfectly clear that it's all over between us. So, say no more. I'll be dressed to kill this coming Friday night, and I hope Taffy is so jealous she tries to gouge my eyes out! Unsuccessfully, of course!"

"Thanks, Kelsey," Cal said, gently squeezing my hand. "You're wonderful."

"Now if only J.P. thought so!" I said with a mocking grin and quickly got out of the car and raced into my house. End of fiasco one. Would the Sno-Ball turn into fiasco two for both Cal and *me*?

✳ thirteen

"You're a miracle worker!" my brother said on the phone Sunday night. He called to share the great news that Priska fell for her own little tricks and was jealously trying to wiggle back into his good graces. "Don't do it, Michael," I pleaded with him. "She's not worth all the trouble!" But I could tell my older brother still had his own lesson to learn.

"You're a miracle worker!" my parents repeated, after learning that Michael planned on staying in school and buckling down.

"You're a miracle worker!" Taffy Foster cried delightedly, after I developed all the prints of the basketball game and pinned them up on the yearbook board.

"Hey, Taffy, these are great!" J.P. commended her, studying the shots. "Taffy did take these, didn't she?" he asked me.

I watched the cheerleader's mouth working nervously behind J.P.'s shoulder, her eyes pleading with mine. "Oh, what the heck!" I grumbled, and nodded sourly. Somehow my desire for revenge had taken a hike in the last few days. The only really important thing I craved now I couldn't have: J.P.'s love and friendship.

He treated me civilly and politely, but was oh-so-heartbreakingly distant. I kept praying that a miracle *would* happen, and I'd get a phone call from John Perry, asking me to meet him and talk. But although I kept Mags off the phone every evening, no romantic reconciliation occurred. And remembering how J.P.'s face looked when he handed me the MMG notebook, I refused to seek him out and initiate a conversation myself. No, if it were really over, I'd better try to forget about John Perry Curtin and the wonderful feeling we once shared.

I could start at the Sno-Ball.

On Friday night, January 14, the Crestwood Country Club was magically transformed for Balboa's winter formal. An elegant building to begin with, it took on *Gone With the Wind* romantic overtones after our decorating committee finished with it. The colonial-style two-wing house with gracious front balconied portico and pillars seemed to sparkle in the evening twilight as the cars pulled out around the circular drive. Tiny white lights blinked in the shrubbery that framed the entrance and a lantern swung gently from the balcony, giving the scene a movie-set flavor. The only thing missing I thought, as Cal carefully helped me out of his Triumph, was a butler to formally announce each couple at the front door. A long red carpet might have been fun, too!

However, it was spectacular enough with the arriving couples dressed in dazzling white tuxes and rainbow-hued long gowns and the sound of the local rock band filtering out through the open French windows. I wanted to get lost in the beauty and the excitement of the evening. I wanted to obliterate all hurtful memories of J.P. and concentrate instead on the tall, smashing creature walking in alongside me. I wanted to . . . but I couldn't. By some ironic twist of fate, just as Cal and I were entering the elegant double front doors leading into the club's foyer, J.P. and Taffy were heading straight at us from the main dancing area! My heart began thudding irregularly and my breathing quickened as Taffy waggled perfectly manicured fingers at Cal and J.P. frowned a distracted hello in our direction.

"How's the band?" Cal raised his voice in order to be heard, and Taffy giggled.

"Terrific. We'll have to dance later—that is, if Kelsey doesn't mind my taking you away from her." Her malicious almond-slanted eyes narrowed at me, but I was beyond her barbs. All the cattiness in the world couldn't hurt me as deeply as seeing J.P.'s arm around her slim waist.

I avoided his eyes and mumbled, "Fine. Anytime you two want."

Cal squeezed my hand in a silent yet happy thanks, and we deposited my wrap at the side cloakroom. I had dressed extra carefully for this evening, as I needed to look as pretty as possible so I could radiate an inner confidence and gaiety I certainly didn't feel. I wore a sleeveless black long gown with a sheer voile patterned wrap that I tucked casually around my bare shoulders and let trail seductively along my waist. The outfit was sensational because it highlighted my hair and eyes and slimmed me considerably. I had shed maybe three or four pounds these past few weeks, and yet, I *felt* much slimmer.

Naturally Cal looked fantastic, a fifteen on a scale of one to ten. It's funny. When I didn't know him personally, I only saw the macho squint and smile that made him ecstatically sexy. Now, after commiserating for hours with him about our troubled love lives, I focused on his little boy vulnerability and kind behavior. So, sure, I could still appreciate his crisp white tux that made him look like a magazine model, but now I only wanted to protect him from Taffy Foster. She was silly and selfish. Cal was open, trusting, and smitten. He'd be hurt and discarded by her as soon as she tired of him. But I couldn't tell him that. It would only make her all the more dangerous and therefore enticing.

What fools guys are! I sighed to myself and then shook the negative thought from my mind. I wouldn't let Priska's cynical philosophy color my own thinking. I had had quite enough of her conniving ways and devious tricks to last me a lifetime. If I could have, I would have taken the little notebook and publicly burned it on J.P.'s front lawn. A trifle dramatic, I suppose, but still indicative of how deep my feelings against Magic Male Grabbers were.

The voting for the king took place around nine. Mr. Del Maio and Mrs. Malachi sat at a small side table and counted the ballots. In ten minutes, Mr. Del Maio cleared his throat and asked for quiet. Cal Lindsey had been elected King of the Sno-Ball! There was an instant thundering of applause, in which I enthusiastically joined. Cal flushed and stood up. Before he went onstage, he leaned over and hugged me. "It's up to you now," I whispered to him. "Go get her!"

He and I knew exactly how essential securing the kingship was in our mutual plans. Because now Cal could select his queen from the five princesses who sat nervously twittering on a dais on the stage. And naturally, Taffy Foster had been chosen one of the five reigning beauties. Although she had been treating Cal coolly, I now saw her eyes gleam and watched a small pointed cat-tongue lick her lips in anticipation.

I let my eyes scan the room and located J.P. He was lounging in a chair, an untouched drink before him on the table, looking bored and unhappy about the whole affair. I stared at him for a few seconds before he felt my gaze and turned to look at me. It was a weird gaze, almost as if I were invisible and he were looking right through me. I flushed hotly and wrenched my gaze away, back to the stage where Cal had picked up the queen's crown and had advanced to the microphone.

There was a sudden hush over the room as the band played a drumroll. Cal flashed a warm, almost intimate smile at me, and I smiled back happily.

"Ladies and gentlemen," he began in that strong voice, "faculty members and administration, my faithful subjects all, I thank you for choosing me as your king. It's an honor, and well, I'm really pleased. If I remember correctly, I now get to select my queen for tonight's dance. And I guess you all know what the requirements are for that. But I want to do something different in choosing the queen. As king, I hope I have some royal authority. There's a certain girl out there tonight who's not one of the princesses, but who's attractive, warm, and special." He lifted the twinkling crown high, cleared his throat and said, "I hereby select KELSEY MARSHALL to be Queen of the Sno-Ball. And these five beautiful princesses to be her entourage for the remainder of the evening."

The drums pounded, the band went wild and the kids in the large ballroom cheered. I couldn't speak. I was too stunned to understand what Cal had done. And when it hit me, I felt scared and yet proud to walk slowly up to the stage and join him. Out of the corner of my eye, I could see Taffy struggling to maintain a wavering smile, but tears shimmered in her eyes. Poor Taffy, I thought. This was probably the first time she had ever been passed over in a beauty contest of any kind and to lose out to her archenemy, the Pig Woman, was shame indeed.

Cal grinned at me like a joyous little kid. "Well, well. Hi, Queen Kelsey," he whispered.

"I don't understand, Cal," I murmured rapidly. "We had it all planned. You were going to choose Taffy."

He shushed me, held the crown up dramatically, and intoned in the microphone, "I hereby crown Kelsey Marshall Queen of the Sno-Ball!"

The crown fit beautifully around my short, layered hair. Mr. Del Maio called out from the side of the stage, "Will you two do us the honor of leading the next dance?"

Cal took my hand and led me down the steps. A soft spotlight played on the empty dance floor and when the band went into a romantic, slow number, we moved into each other's arms and glided off into a fantasy world of our own. In the back of my mind, I could hear the clapping and appreciative whistles following our progress, but basically I was in dreamland, a wonderful colorful spot I knew I'd cherish for the rest of my life. It's not every day a girl becomes a queen and gets to move in a hazy romantic fog to music and colored lights, beamed only at her—and her partner.

"Cal, you've got to explain this to me!" I demanded, pushing slightly away from him.

He relaxed his grip and shook his head. "Just enjoy it. I wanted you to be singled out and honored for once. Not the cheerleaders or the other bubble-brained princesses. But you."

"But what about Taffy?"

"What about her? Stop worrying about her. She worries enough about herself for everyone combined. She needs to realize that being nice to people is more important than being pretty. I can still get turned on by Taffy's looks but I won't get suckered into her games. If she wants to date me, she has to stop acting like a selfish little girl."

A great sigh escaped me. "Oh Cal! How'd you learn so much—so fast?"

"Easy!" he retorted with a flash of his dimples. "From hanging around you!"

We finished the dance in a companionable silence. But I couldn't help thinking how perfect it all would be if J.P. were in my arms. When the music faded to be replaced by a fast set, I backed away from Cal with an apologetic grin.

"Uneasy lies the head that wears the crown and dances too fast!" I paraphrased. "I'm going to the girls' room for a second. Dance your little heart away, O king, while I retire to yon throne room."

I gave him a mock salute, grabbed my bag from the table, and headed for the bathroom. Once inside I was surrounded by admiring girls who wanted to check out the value of the crown I was wearing. Flushed and happy, I repaired my eye shadow, combed my hair oh-so-carefully around the crown, and came back to the main ballroom to discover a serious king talking animatedly with J.P. Curtin near the refreshment table! Whatever they were discussing was pretty hot and heavy, I felt, because neither one cracked a smile in the length of time it took me to wend my way slowly to the table and sit down. I was uneasy, but quickly turned my head away when Taffy and two of the princesses walked up to me. Taffy stared at me sullenly, but the other two girls smiled and introduced themselves. We chatted amiably for a few minutes about how great the dance was. Then I finally looked directly into Taffy's eyes and smiled at her. I was so happy at that point, I just couldn't help it. It was a genuine smile, too, though mostly composed of pity that we wasted half a school year hating each other so much. She didn't smile back, but the anger in her eyes wavered, flickered into uncertainty.

"You look beautiful," I told her. "You really do."

After giving me a confused stare, she dropped her eyes and mumbled, "Thanks." Then she led the two girls to another table. Taffy and I would never be friends. I frowned, but I didn't expect miracles. I would continue to be pleasant and see what would happen. I sighed, then yelped in surprise when a cold drink was pressed lightly against my shoulder blades. A grinning Cal handed me the concoction with a slight bow, and I growled at him unconvincingly.

"Listen, Kelsey," he said, leaning down with a serious expression on his face, "would you mind if I danced with Taffy? Cindy told me on the sly how much Taffy wants to dance with me, but is too embarrassed to come up and ask me!"

"Sounds great! Maybe she's really learned a lesson. Enjoy yourself. And Cal, don't worry about me."

His answering smile was mysterious. "Oh, I know, I know. I won't have to worry about you the rest of the evening."

Now what in heaven's name was all that about? I frowned, taking a sip of the drink and glancing over at the dance floor. I scanned the refreshment table, too, and the two doorways, but couldn't find the object of my search. Oh no, J.P.'s gone! He's taken off for the evening. Taffy's floating angelically around the floor in Cal's arms, and J.P. probably got fed up and packed it in. I put my drink down abruptly and was about to rise when a hand on my arm stopped me.

"J.P.!" I exclaimed. He sat down beside me. His grip on my

arm was gentle, but the expression on his face was *not*. I swallowed nervously and wrapped the voile shawl more tightly around my shoulders. Was there a definite chill in the air, or did it emanate directly from the dark stranger who sat glowering at me? But in the next second I forgot the chilly climate when J.P. leaned dangerously close to me, slid his warm hands on my bare shoulders and touched my lips in the gentlest, most sensitive kiss I could ever imagine! I pulled away instinctively, but my mouth was still tingling and my heartbeat zoomed immediately to 120 miles per hour.

"Well," I stammered, searching his mysterious eyes, "what was that all about, that—that—"

"What?" he grinned and pulled me close again. "You mean this?" And leaned down and kissed my lips again, only this time with even more feeling. At the end of the kiss, I gave up struggling and laid my head securely against his shoulder. I was sure he could hear the pounding of my heart, but I didn't care. I was sure I could hear the pounding of his.

"Oh, Kelsey," he whispered, gently stroking my fingers, "I've wanted to do that for so long. But you wouldn't let me."

"I wouldn't let you?" I gaped at him, then giggled. "*You* were the one who was always playing hard to get, you with Taffy Foster. It drove me crazy. It drove me—"

"Right into Cal's arms? I know, Kelsey, he set me straight tonight and told me the whole story. How you and he played the little love match to get me and Taffy jealous. That was a really dumb thing to do, Marshall. D-U-M. And you're normally a pretty smart cookie. Didn't you realize how much I liked you the afternoon I kissed you at your house? I like you just the way you are, no lies, no games, just you being you." His fingers left my hand and gently pushed a wisp of my hair out of my dazed, happy eyes. "Those Magic Male Grabbers

132

made you change into a girl I didn't know or trust anymore. Suddenly, it wasn't Kelsey but a—but a—"

"Clone doll of Cotton Candy?" I supplied, and we both fell over laughing.

"Well," he accused me with a twinkle, "didn't you honestly start to feel like her? Ever?"

I sobered up quickly and nodded at Cal and Taffy dancing. "You see that?" I asked. "That girl is a perfect example of a programmed doll, all programmed to flirt and lie and twist the truth to get what she wants. And I realized tonight just how unhappy she is. And do you know why? Because she can never be herself. J.P., I don't think Taffy Foster even knows herself, I mean, as a person."

"She doesn't like herself either." J.P. shook his head. "The little time I spent with her told me that all too clearly. But you, Kelsey, now you're a different story altogether. One I want to read and reread everyday for a long, long time. What do you say, can we begin a new chapter tonight, just the two of us?"

"Oh, John Perry, I'd love that! I'm crazy about you!" I blurted out, throwing away Magic Male Grabbers forever. If it feels this good to be honest, then I'll take honest any day.

And J.P. seemed to confirm my decision by hugging me tightly and looking at me with a glow on his face. "That's great! Because it just so happens I'm bonkers over you, too!"

We kissed one more sizzling time, and then I pulled away and searched his gorgeous face with a faint trace of suspicion. "Wait a minute. Since we're being open and honest now, what's this about Amy Lanier and the Sadie Hawkins Dance?"

"Amy Lanier?" J.P. frowned, squinting in furious concentration.

"Yes, the Amy Lanier who danced so closely with you that the fire department had to be alerted."

His face cleared, and I could have sworn a tiny smile popped up in his eyes, but his mouth was perfectly serious. "Oh, *that* Amy Lanier. Well, you know, Marshall, it was all so long ago, and a certain someone wasn't even looking at me *then,* and I felt hurt and a little down when that certain someone didn't show at the dance so I— Well, let's just say that a man's entitled to a few secrets in his past, isn't he?"

"Why you, you—" I stammered in frustration and began mock punching him. We both started roaring with laughter, and it was then I thought I heard J.P. whisper to himself, "MMG #37? Or was that #38?" But it all flew out of my mind when he gently pulled me close and began kissing me again.